A Shower of Roses

Also by Tom Milton

Infamy
All the Flowers
The Admiral's Daughter
No Way to Peace

A Shower of Roses

Tom Milton

NEPPERHAN PRESS, LLC
YONKERS, NY

Published by Nepperhan Press, LLC
P.O. Box 1448, Yonkers, NY 10702
nepperhan@optonline.net
nepperhan.com

PUBLISHER'S NOTE
This is a work of fiction. Names, characters, places, and incidents
are the product of the author's imagination or are used fictitiously,
and any resemblance to actual persons, living or dead, events, or
locales is entirely coincidental.

Printed in the United States of America

Library of Congress Control Number: 2010915636

ISBN 978-0-9829904-1-4

Cover art was licensed from Publitek, Inc.

For Marie

"I will spend my heaven doing good on earth.
I will let fall a shower of roses."

St. Thérèse of Lisieux, *The Story of a Soul*

London, 1981

ONE

AS SHE WALKED along Park Lane in the benign warmth of the April sun, Eva was worried. Her husband, Marek, had been in Poland for five days, and she hadn't heard from him since the night he arrived there.

Of course it was hard to make a phone call, but if he had tried, really tried, he could have gotten through to her. So she was vacillating between her fear that something had happened to him and her fear that he didn't care enough to try to call her.

Immediately she blamed herself for questioning his love for her, and in the end she was stranded with the fear that something had happened to him.

She wouldn't have been so worried if she hadn't known that the ostensible purpose of his trip, to collect information for his bank, was a cover for the real purpose, to collect information for the CIA. And now, for a moment, she wished he hadn't told her. She wished she was blissfully ignorant of what he was really doing in Poland.

But if he hadn't told her, they wouldn't have had an honest relationship. They would have had a marriage in which one of the parties was deceiving the other, and neither of them wanted that. They wanted to be completely honest with each other and to share everything that happened in their lives, believing that trust and sharing were the foundations of marital love. And though it caused her heartache, she preferred to know the truth about what her husband was doing.

Approaching Hyde Park Corner, she tried to figure out how to get to the other side of Knightsbridge Road. She had been in London almost three months, but she had spent most of that time furnishing their apartment, trying to make a home for Marek, so she was just beginning to know her way around.

She made a guess and followed people into an underpass. Emerging where she wanted to be, she felt proud of herself. She strode along Knightsbridge, entered Brompton Road, passed Harrods, and turned into Beauchamp Place, which she had pronounced the French way until Juliana corrected her. They were meeting for lunch at a Portuguese restaurant on this street. Juliana was feeling homesick for her native country, Brazil, and since she hadn't found any Brazilian restaurants in London, she was hoping to soothe that feeling with the closest thing.

Eva went into the restaurant cautiously, not knowing what to expect, and she was relieved to see Juliana seated at a table where you couldn't miss her. Head waiters always sat her in the place of honor, assuming she was a celebrity, and people always stared at her, believing they had seen her in a film or a magazine but not remembering who she was. She was great to go to restaurants with because she always got the royal treatment.

Eva had met Juliana at a party given by the man at the bank whom Marek reported to. Juliana came with her husband, Adrian, whose firm did legal work for the bank. The two women were the same age and the same height, and they had almost the same hair, eye, and skin color, so they could have been taken for sisters. They looked Italian, but Juliana was half Italian and half Portuguese, while Eva was a hundred percent Polish.

Juliana had lived in London for about three years, so she knew her way around, and she was Eva's guide to the city as well as her companion when Marek was away.

"Are you okay?" Juliana asked after they had exchanged kisses of greeting on both cheeks.

"I'm fine," Eva said, sitting down.

"You look worried."

"I always worry when Marek's away."

"What do you worry about?"

"Everything. That his plane might crash, that his driver might have an accident." She couldn't tell her friend she worried that

Marek would be arrested, tortured, and killed. It would have sounded crazy since such things didn't happen to bankers.

"It doesn't do any good to worry," Juliana said. "It won't stop anything bad from happening."

"I know it won't," Eva agreed. "It's better to pray."

"I do that often. I pray that the military won't harm my brothers and sisters."

Juliana's father was an obstetrician in Rio de Janeiro whose only interest beyond his family was in helping women give birth to healthy babies, so the military wouldn't harm his children because of anything he had done. The problem was that his children, starting with Juliana, had gotten involved in politics as students at the university. For her safety Juliana's father had sent her to the Villard School in New York, where she had become fully committed to being a musician.

The waiter brought menus, which they didn't look at.

"I finally got the application," Eva said, referring to the first step in the process of getting registered as a nurse.

"It only took them two months," Juliana said ironically.

"At that rate it'll take me two years to get registered. But it's partly my fault. I should have brought my documents with me."

"What documents do they need?"

"To start the process, they need my birth certificate, my nursing license, my marriage certificate, my college transcripts, my nursing experience, and my professional references, all of them certified, notarized, and stamped."

"That's just to start the process?"

"Yeah. You don't want to hear the rest of it. So it'll take me at least a year to get registered."

The waiter returned, and Juliana ordered a bottle of *vinho verde.*

"I miss working," Eva said. "I've never been idle, and I don't know what to do with my time."

"Pretend you're a tourist and get to know London," Juliana advised. "Because once you start working, you won't have time for anything else."

"I guess I won't."

"As soon as my harpsichord arrived from Rio, I didn't have time for anything else."

"How many hours a day do you practice?"

"About eight. But I always take a break for lunch. It's one of the customs I brought from my country."

"So you miss your country."

"I miss my family. And I miss some things about my country. But I don't miss living under a military government."

"Well, maybe they won't be in power much longer."

"They will be as long as America supports them. You know," Juliana explained, "the CIA helped to install them. The CIA prefers military governments."

This reference to the CIA made Eva uncomfortable. She was deceiving Juliana by not telling her Marek worked for the CIA, but she couldn't tell her. So instead of pursuing the conversation, she looked at her menu, which was written in Portuguese and English, and not knowing what to order, she asked: "What do you recommend?"

"Any kind of fish," Juliana told her.

"What are you having?"

"*Bacalhau à Gomes de Sá.* It's salt cod with potatoes and onions. It's comfort food."

"You think I should try it?"

"You can taste mine. Have the fresh cod. You'll like that."

The waiter brought a bottle of wine, opened it, poured a little for Juliana to taste, and after her approval poured two glasses. Then he took their food orders.

"Well, I found something to do in the meantime," Eva said when the waiter had left them. "I'm going to take a postgraduate course in developmental psychology."

"You are? Where?"

"At Birkbeck."

"Will you have day classes or evening classes?"

"Evening classes. But I'll have to study during the day, so that'll help me fill the time."

"When do classes start?"

"The week after next. The term runs until early July."

"This could be an opportunity," Juliana said. "It could lead you into a new specialty."

"What do you mean?"

"Psychiatric nursing. There's a strong demand for it. And it would be especially useful for you."

Eva got the joke. Since her friend believed that Marek was crazy, a specialty in psychiatric nursing would be useful for her personally as well as professionally. "I don't want to go into that field. I love pediatric nursing. And if I had a choice, I wouldn't study psychology. I'd practice my profession."

"Sometimes it's good not to have a choice," Juliana reflected. "If I'd had a choice, I might not have gone to New York to study. I might not have followed my passion for music."

"What about your passion for politics?"

"I was involved in politics, but I didn't have a passion for it. That's how your husband and I are different. He has a passion for politics."

"How do you know?"

"From the way he talked that night you came to dinner. I mean, about the communist government in Poland. He sounded like he was involved in the situation."

"He does have a passion for politics," Eva admitted warily, "and he is involved in the situation. But he's not involved in politics. He's only a banker."

"When countries have borrowed a lot of money, bankers are always involved in politics. They want governments that will pay back their loans."

"Well, he's only collecting information from the government. He's not trying to overthrow it."

"But he's not happy with the situation."

"No. His dream is an independent Poland, with a democratic government."

"That was Chopin's dream."

"He admires Chopin, and Kościuszko, and Pulaski—all the heroes who had the dream of an independent Poland."

"They all failed to achieve their dream."

"At least they had a dream."

Juliana nodded and solemnly said: "I had a dream. My dream was an independent Brazil, with a democratic government. But trying to achieve that dream was like trying to ram my head through a wall. And that's what your husband is doing—trying to ram his head through a wall."

"He has a hard head," Eva said lightly.

"You should know," Juliana said, smiling.

After lunch they parted, with Juliana heading toward Cadogan Square and Eva heading toward Brompton Road. She considered taking the tube from Knightsbridge, but having no further engagements that day and seeing no rain clouds in the sky, she decided to walk.

She walked to Hyde Park Corner and then along Park Lane, which she left at Curzon Street. She walked along South Audley Street toward Grosvenor Square. From time to time she still had to consult the guide that she carried in her handbag, but between glances at the map she didn't take any wrong turns.

As she walked she thought about her conversation with Juliana, especially the parts about Marek, and she acknowledged that her friend had intuited something essential about her husband. He was trying to achieve an impossible dream. He was driven by that dream, which at some level meant more to him than anything in the world. She had known this when she fell in love with him. It might have been a reason why she fell in love with him. She admired his commitment to something larger than himself. She believed he operated at a higher level than she did since she was concerned with babies and children, who played no immediate role in changing the world.

Yet he respected what she did professionally, and he often said that her work was far more important than his. He had even tried to use the bank's influence to cut through the bureaucratic regulations that stopped her from working as a nurse in London.

And he had promised to keep trying since he expected to stay in London for a while.

She crossed Oxford Street and headed up Duke Street to Manchester Square, where she briefly considered visiting the Wallace Collection but then was impelled by a need stronger than the solace of art to continue walking to George Street and into the church of St. James.

As the door closed behind her the hectic sounds of the city were silenced, the light was dimmed, and the air was stilled. This was her sanctuary, her refuge from a world of hatred and war. This was where she felt at home, where she found a world of love and peace.

She dipped her fingers into the stoup and blessed herself and went into the nave. She stopped for a moment and gazed in awe at the high vaulted arches that with the light filtered through the stained-glass windows created for her an uplifting space where she palpably felt the presence of God.

Then she went to the Lady Chapel, which she had discovered on her first visit to the church. She knelt at the rail and happily fixed her eyes on *The Immaculate Conception*, a copy of a painting by Murillo that according to its history the church had received from a Spanish count. She loved the painting, which showed the Virgin Mary as she had always imagined her—pure and modest and warm and kind.

With all her heart she prayed to the Blessed Mother, asking her to bring Marek home safely and to lead him to salvation. For a moment Mary's face was obliterated by Marek's face, and she was looking into the abyss of his dark eyes. The plight of that baby abandoned by his mother pierced her heart, and she prayed until his eyes were transformed, infused by the faith that radiated from Mary's eyes. She renewed her vow to love her husband no matter what he did, and she reaffirmed her belief that she could heal his heart, restore his faith, and save his soul.

After blessing herself she rose to her feet and left the church, no longer worried.

She walked along George Street to Manchester Street and turned left. She crossed Blandford Street, which was busy as usual, and arrived in the block where after much looking they had found an apartment. It was on the second floor of a four-story townhouse that had been converted to apartments, or flats, as they called them here. The ground floor had a stone veneer with decorative elements, and the front door was painted red. Above the ground floor the face of the building was brown brick, with iron grates at the bottoms of the windows that suggested balconies.

Climbing the stairs to the second floor she had a feeling of anticipation, and she quickened her pace. She unlocked the door to the apartment and opened it, immediately seeing on the floor ahead of her Marek's beat-up leather bag.

She thanked the Blessed Mother for answering her prayer.

Then she hurried into the kitchen, where she found Marek pouring himself a shot of vodka.

He put down the bottle and opened his arms, and Eva flew into them. They hugged each other for dear life, as if it was a miracle that they were together.

"I missed you so much," she told him, inhaling the smell of his aftershave.

"I missed you too," he said with equal passion.

"I was worried when I didn't hear from you."

"I tried to call you a number of times, but the phones don't work there. It's a third-world country," he added with scorn. "The communists can't do anything right."

She pulled back and looked at his face. She saw a light in his dark eyes that hadn't been there in the image she had seen in church. She knew it came from his love for her. And it confirmed her belief that she could save him.

"Would you like some vodka?" he asked her.

"Sure. Let's sit down, and you can tell me about your trip."

She let go of him so that he could finish pouring the vodka, and then she took her glass and led him into the living room.

They sat on the sofa, maintaining body contact. She kicked off her shoes and drew up her legs and leaned against him, sipping the vodka.

He put an arm around her and held her close.

"So what's happening in Poland?" she asked him.

"A lot," he told her. "Things are going from bad to worse."

"Will the government default on its debt?"

"Technically, it already has. But we're all trying to make it look like an orderly restructuring."

"Why don't you just admit the truth?"

"Because the truth is frightening. The banks are afraid they'll have to write off a lot of bad loans, and the Russians are afraid they'll be cut off from Western credit."

"What about the government?"

"They're not afraid of defaulting. They realize that when you owe a lot of money, you have the bankers by the balls."

"I had lunch with Juliana today," she said, remembering their conversation. "She thinks you're involved in politics."

"She hasn't guessed what I'm doing, has she?"

"No. She hasn't. She says that when countries have borrowed a lot of money, bankers are always involved in politics. They want governments that will pay back their loans."

"Well, they do want that. But they're not trying to change the government. They're just trying to get the government to manage its finances better."

"That's what I told her. But she's very suspicious of bankers."

"She's a typical leftist," Marek said. "She believes that bankers run the world."

"They do have a lot of influence, don't they?"

"Not as much as people like Juliana believe. If they did, the world would be more orderly."

"Would that be good?"

"If they had too much power, it wouldn't be good. But if I had to choose, I'd rather have bankers running the world than communists."

"You know," Eva said after a silence, "Juliana had the same dream for Brazil that you have for Poland. Her dream was an independent Brazil, with a democratic government."

"What did she mean? Brazil's independent."

"I think she meant that Brazil's under the domination of America just as Poland's under the domination of Russia."

"It's not even remotely the same. America has ideals, and it never did to a country what Russia did to Poland."

"We took a third of Mexico."

"You took a third, but you didn't take the whole country." Though Marek had lived in America since he was fourteen and had become an American citizen, he still thought of himself as Polish, which should have made him objective about America. But he had illusions about the country.

Eva took another sip of vodka. "So the banks aren't trying to change the government. But what about the CIA?"

"We're trying to change it."

She waited for him to explain.

"We're positioning Solidarity to take over."

Solidarity was an independent union founded seven months ago in the Gdańsk Shipyard that had quickly grown into a broad movement against the government installed by Russia. It was supported by the Catholic Church, starting with the Polish pope, and it was committed to nonviolence. "Solidarity? How would they take over?"

"By a peaceful revolution."

"What about the army?"

"If there are ten million people in the streets—men, women, and children—the army won't do anything to oppose them. Polish soldiers won't fire on their own people."

"Russian soldiers would, wouldn't they?"

"Yeah, they would. They fired on the Hungarians, and they fired on the Czechs. They'd fire on their own grandmothers."

"So the Russians could stop a peaceful revolution."

"Your government has warned them not to intervene."

"But what if they did intervene?" she asked. "Would that start World War III?"

"Why not? An invasion of Poland started World War II."

"We let the Russians go into Hungary and into Czechoslovakia. Why wouldn't we let them go into Poland?"

"You're in a different situation," Marek explained. "You know the Russians aren't as powerful as you thought they were, and there are a lot more Poles in America than Hungarians or Czechs, so there would be a lot more support for standing up to the Russians this time."

"Support for going to war?"

"Yes. Sooner or later you're going to war with Russia, and this would be a good time. Almost as good as the time you should have stopped Russia from taking over Poland."

He was referring to the period following World War II when Russia took over Eastern Europe with the acquiescence of the West. It was a sore subject, and Eva had heard it discussed endlessly in the Polish community where she had grown up. They loved America, and they were super-patriots, but at the same time they blamed America for not pushing the Russians back where they belonged.

"If the Russians get the message," Eva said, gazing into the distance, "and they don't send troops into Poland, then what can stop Solidarity?"

"Nothing can stop them—unless Jaruzelski disables them before they can organize a revolution."

Jaruzelski was the Russian puppet prime minister of Poland. He was also minister of defense, a position he had occupied since 1968. At that time he had led the Polish troops who helped the Russians crush the revolt in Czechoslovakia known as the Prague Spring, and ten years ago he had organized the suppression of the revolt in Poland, which resulted in massacres of striking workers in Gdynia and Szczecin. "How could he disable them?"

"By rounding up their leaders in the middle of the night."

"Can he do that?" Eva asked.

"He can," Marek said, "if he becomes a military dictator. Look at what happened in Brazil and Chile and Argentina. The same thing could happen in Poland."

"Juliana said that the CIA prefers military governments."

"We prefer them to communist governments. But in Poland there's an opportunity for a democratic government that your country would support. So we want to stop Jaruzelski from becoming a military dictator."

"And that's what you're doing in Poland?"

"Right. We're trying to stop that *pieprzony sukinsyn*."

"But how can you stop him?"

"By acting before he does. We have a source that's close to him," Marek explained, "and we know he's afraid to do anything unless the Russians agree to support him by sending in troops. And we know they haven't agreed to do that. So we have time to act before he does."

"If the Russians don't agree to send in troops, might Jaruzelski act anyway?"

"He might. So we don't have much time."

"Why don't you act now?"

"We're not ready," Marek said. "We won't be ready for a few more months."

She saw what was coming, and she was dismayed. "When do you have to go back to Poland?"

"Next week. I'm sorry."

She put down her glass and moved into a position where she could give him an inviting kiss.

They slept late the next morning, and Marek didn't leave for work until noon. She was hoping they would have the evening all to themselves, but around three he called and told her he was bringing Lukasz and Czeslaw home for dinner. She was disappointed, but she went out and bought a pork roast, potatoes, carrots, and sauerkraut, enough to feed eight people since she knew how much the two young men were capable of eating. And it did give her a kind of maternal satisfaction to feed a pair of starving students.

When they arrived with her husband she could hear them talking on the stairs. As always they were talking in Polish.

"*Dobry wieczór,*" Lukasz said to her, coming in the door. He was big and blond with blue eyes and pink cheeks like Eva's brothers. "*Dziękuje za gościnność.*"

"*Przyjemność jest moja,*" she said, acknowledging his thanks for her hospitality.

"Good evening," Czeslaw said to her, handing her a rumpled paper bag. He was short and dark like Eva, and he wore glasses with black rims. "These are homemade *chruściki.*"

They knew how much she loved *chruściki*, the ribbons of crisp fried dough sprinkled with confectioner's sugar. When you ate them you ended up with sugar all over you from the tip of your nose to the lap of your skirt.

"*Dziękuja,*" Eva said, taking the bag. She gave Czeslaw a kiss on a cheek.

"How come he gets a kiss and I don't?" Lukasz asked good-naturedly.

"He's easier to reach," Marek said, referring to the fact that Czeslaw was shorter.

Eva rose to her tiptoes and kissed Lukasz on a pink cheek.

"That's better," Lukasz said, turning pinker.

"Would you like some vodka?" Marek asked them.

"*Tak, proszę,*" the two young men said almost together.

"Please sit down," she told them, motioning to the sofa. She had timed the dinner for eight o'clock since she knew they would want to talk for at least two hours before eating.

She took the bag of *chruściki* into the kitchen and set it on the counter. She watched Marek get the bottle of vodka out of the freezing compartment of the refrigerator where he always kept it. Then he got out four of their Polish crystal shot glasses.

They each carried two of the glasses, filled to within a half inch of the top, into the living room. Eva handed a glass to each of the young men, and Marek handed a glass to her.

"*Na zdrowie!*" he said, raising his glass.

"*Na zdrowie!*" Lukasz said.

"*Sto lat!*" Czeslaw said.

The three men downed the vodka in one gulp, while Eva sipped hers.

Then Marek took one of the chairs opposite the sofa, and she took the other, ready to listen as always to their conversation. She rarely made a comment. She was fluent in Polish since it had been her first language, but she didn't always understand what they were talking about.

Lukasz and Czeslaw were experts on the subject. They were leaders of militant student organizations respectively in Warsaw and Krakow. They had been in Gdańsk at a meeting to form a coalition between students and workers when an informer, revealing himself as a member of the secret police, tried to arrest them. Seeing no choice, they killed the man. They escaped from Poland and became political refugees in London. That happened several months ago, and since they had known Marek from Poland they contacted him and started working with him here. They still had contacts, they still had methods of communication, and they still had influence. In fact, they were even more highly respected for having killed a police spy.

When she looked at them Eva was struck by the fact that they were just kids, who could have been her younger brothers. Yet they had killed a man.

"From what I hear," Lukasz said, "I think we have at least six months before Jaruzelski takes over."

"I don't agree," Czeslaw said. "I think we have no more than three months."

"If that's the case," Marek said, "we have to be ready by July."

"Well, the students are ready," Lukasz said.

"And the workers are ready," Czeslaw said. "At least the ones who belong to Solidarity."

"But that's not enough," Marek said. "We need ten million people in the streets."

"How did you get that number?" Lukasz asked.

"It's enough to overwhelm the army."

"With half that number you could overwhelm the army."

"You'd still have the police," Czeslaw said.

"The police couldn't arrest ten million people," Marek argued.

"They don't have to. They only have to arrest the leaders."

"They almost got us," Lukasz said.

"But they didn't get you," Marek said. "And they won't get the other leaders."

"How will we stop them?"

"We'll protect the leaders like they do in America."

"You mean with secret service agents?"

"They didn't do a very good job protecting the Kennedys," Czeslaw pointed out.

"They've tightened up security since then," Marek said.

"Maybe they have for your presidents, but they haven't for the pope. And that worries me."

"You really think the Russians would assassinate the pope?" Lukasz asked as if he couldn't imagine it.

"They have a good reason to," Czeslaw said. "The pope has supported our movement from the very beginning."

"Well, I'm sure they're protecting him."

"How can they protect him? He's out in the open."

"I'll pray for his safety," Eva said, making a rare comment. She knew that Marek wouldn't pray for the pope's safety since he was an avowed atheist.

"It's the job of the Swiss Guards to protect the pope," Marek said. "We need the equivalent to protect our leaders."

"The ideal people," Czeslaw said, "would be defectors from the police."

"I agree," Lukasz said. "But how do we find them?"

"We look for them," Marek said. "But in the meantime we should recruit guards from the students. There must be students who know how to use weapons."

"We'll find them," Czeslaw said.

"We could also recruit guards from the workers," Lukasz said.

"Now, let's go back," Marek said, "to the ten million people we need in the streets."

"Would you settle for five million?" Czeslaw asked.

"If our leaders are protected, yes. But in order to get that number, we need more people on board. For one thing, we need more older people."

"You mean people over thirty?"

"Yeah. And over forty."

"You can't trust people over thirty."

"I don't know if you can trust them," Lukasz said, "but they don't want to take any risks."

"They don't," Czeslaw agreed. "They're comfortable in the present situation."

"How the hell can they be comfortable?" Marek asked. "The country's broke. And the government wants to raise food prices. How will people eat?"

"They think America will rescue them," Lukasz said.

"We have to get the message to older people," Marek said, "that America won't rescue them unless they're in the streets trying to overthrow a communist government."

"America won't rescue them whatever they do," Czeslaw said. "It didn't rescue Hungary or Czechoslovakia."

"Poland is different. Poland is the key country in the Cold War. If the communist government in Poland falls, then all the other communist governments will fall, including the communist government in Russia."

"That sounds like a domino theory," Lukasz said.

"It is," Marek said, "but it's a valid one."

"I agree with the domino theory," Czeslaw said. "But I have doubts about America. I mean, if older people in Poland are so comfortable that they won't get off their asses to overthrow an evil government, why would Americans get off their asses to rescue us? No people are more comfortable than Americans."

"You don't know them," Marek said.

"You really think that if the Russians sent troops into Poland, the Americans would intervene?"

"I think they would."

"What do you think?" Czeslaw asked Eva.

The question surprised her. "I don't know. I guess they would. But I wouldn't bet my life on it."

"I wouldn't either."

"If we overthrow the government," Marek maintained, "the Americans will be the first to recognize the new government. And they won't let the Russians touch it."

"If the Russians don't send troops into Poland," Lukasz said, "I think the Americans will support us."

"They've warned the Russians not to send in troops," Marek reminded them.

"All right. Let's go for it," Czeslaw said.

By eight they were ready for dinner, which Eva served with bottles of red Rhone wine. The eight-pound pork roast was reduced to a pile of bones, while the potatoes, carrots, and sauerkraut completely disappeared.

While eating, the young men broke the silence only to say things like *"Kapusta jest bardzo dobra"* and *"Wieprzowina jest bardzo dobra,"* meaning that the sauerkraut was very good and the pork was very good. And Eva was pleased. Their compliments meant a lot to her, and she felt that she owed it to their mothers to feed them well.

For dessert she put the *chruściki* on a plate and passed it around. As usual, she ended up with sugar all over her, including the front of her sweater where it bulged out. These spots of sugar had not gone unnoticed by Lukasz, who no doubt would have been more than willing to brush them off. She smiled, wondering if the two young men had found any Polish girls in London. They had to be as lonely as they were hungry.

They helped her clear the table and offered to help her with the dishes, but she sent them back to the living room, where they joined Marek for an after-dinner drink of brandy. They were still talking, but winding down, when she finished the dishes and joined them.

Before sitting down with them, she wandered over to the

window and looked out to see what the weather was like. It wasn't raining. In fact, it hadn't rained as much as she had been led to believe it would.

She was about to turn from the window when she noticed two men, who didn't look like neighbors, standing across the street and watching the house.

TWO

HER EARLIEST MEMORY was of her father sitting at a table, looking sad. The table was in the kitchen, and there was a bottle of vodka on it. There was also a half-empty glass.

Her mother was standing at the stove, preparing dinner.

Wanting to make her father happy, she went to him and told him: "Papa, I love you."

He nodded slightly as if he knew this, but he raised his hand and held her off.

She must have been about four at the time.

Years later she learned why he was sad. As a university student he had joined the Armia Krajowa, the main force of the Polish resistance movement against the German occupation. They were the largest such force in Europe, and they provided valuable assistance to the Allied forces in the war against the Germans. Their activities culminated in the Warsaw Uprising, the purpose of which was to liberate the city and deliver it to the Polish government in exile. For more than two months they fought against the German army, which outnumbered them and outgunned them. Bombarding indiscriminately, the Germans reduced the city to rubble and not only destroyed the Armia Krajowa but ruthlessly killed hundreds of thousands of civilians. Those who survived the fighting were sent to concentration camps, where they were systematically annihilated. Eva's father, who survived the battle with a wounded leg, was captured and held by the Germans as a prisoner of war.

Meanwhile, the Russians—supposedly our allies—had halted their forces less than twelve miles outside the city and waited there while the Germans destroyed the only force that could have prevented them from taking over Poland. When the Russians finally marched into Warsaw there was no one left to resist them.

Eva's father, whose camp was overrun by Russian troops, was identified as a member of the Armia Krajowa and classified as a war criminal. They left him in the camp, along with others who might have caused trouble for the new occupiers of Poland, and they scheduled a trial, the outcome of which he knew in advance. At the time he was twenty-three, and he decided he would rather die attempting to escape than be executed, so he and three fellow prisoners seized the opportunity when their Russian guards got drunk on Polish vodka, and they found a way out of the camp. Miraculously, they all made it to West Germany, where they spent another year in an American camp but eventually were released and given passage to New York.

After staying in Greenpoint for a while he moved to St. Paul, where a distant relative who lived in the Polish community there had found him a job at Seeger Refrigerator. He was in America, but his mind was still in Poland.

Eva had heard him talk about the war so many times with men who shared his experience that she could remember their conversations almost verbatim. Typically, they were in the kitchen, four or five men who had come off the eight-to-four shift at the Seeger (now called Whirlpool) plant, still in their work clothes, smelling of sweat and metal and paint, sitting at the table, smoking cigarettes, and drinking Schmidt beer out of brown bottles, while she was at the sink peeling potatoes but ready when asked to get another beer out of the refrigerator.

"*Rosjanie są barbarzyńcy,*" one of the men would invariably say. "Russians are barbarians."

"They have no culture," another man would say. "They haven't even come down from the trees."

"They claim to be Christians, but that's a sham."

"They're not Christians. They're not even pagans."

"A gang of Russian soldiers raped my little sister. I'll never forgive them. If I could line them up, I'd kill every last one of those fuckers."

"They tortured my brother."

"They shot my nephew in cold blood. The kid was only ten years old."

"They haven't changed from the time when Sienkiewicz described them. You know what they did with their captives? They impaled them on stakes."

"Yeah, right through the asshole."

Eva winced. She hoped this wasn't true.

"What I don't understand," her father said, "is why the Americans didn't come to our rescue. Didn't they know what would happen to Poland if they let the Germans wipe us out?"

"They weren't in a position to help us."

"They were. By then they had beaten the Germans."

"I think they expected the Russians to help us. The Russians were in a better position to help us."

"But they should have *known* that the Russians wouldn't help us," her father argued. "They only had to look at history. Russia has always wanted Poland."

"And they've taken it before."

"They want Poland because it has a civilization."

"That's why the Romans wanted Greece."

"At least the Romans evolved into a civilized people. The Russians are never going to evolve. They'll always be barbarians."

"Well, they won't be able to keep Poland forever."

"Why won't they? They have no opposition."

"They still have to deal with the church. They haven't been able to destroy that."

"They will in time. If the church doesn't take a stand against them, it'll lose authority."

"It *has* taken stands. But it hasn't taken a major stand."

"Cardinal Wojtyla will take a major stand."

"No, he won't. Now that he's a cardinal, he'll go along with establishment."

"They say he fought with the resistance in Krakow."

"They all claim they fought with the resistance, even the communists who are sucking blood out of our country."

"Gomulka doesn't claim he fought with the resistance."

"He helped the Russians take over our country."

"He's nothing but a Russian tool."

"So where was your cardinal last March when Gomulka was arresting the students?"

"He was supporting them. But it's against his principles to encourage them to take up arms."

"Cardinal Wojtyla believes in a peaceful revolution," her father said skeptically.

"We'll never have a peaceful revolution. The only way to get the Russians out of Poland is to drive them out by force."

"And who's going to do that? Hubert Humphrey?"

They all laughed. Humphrey, who had made his political career in Minnesota, was now running for president against Richard Nixon.

"We sent a million troops to Vietnam to fight the Russians there. It makes no sense. The Vietnamese aren't even fighting with us."

"Think what we could do with a million troops in Poland. The Poles would fight with us, and together we'd drive those barbarians out of Poland."

The conversations typically ended with this kind of dream.

Eva's mother was a nurse in Poland, and she was ordered by the Germans to care for their wounded. She performed her duty, and she often said there was no difference between a wounded German, a wounded Pole, or a wounded American—they were all poor boys sent to be killed or wounded or mentally damaged by old men who didn't have the courage to lead their armies and risk their lives. She didn't talk about wounded Russians since that would have provoked an argument with Eva's father.

When the war ended she was held in an American camp for a while, and then she had a choice of returning to her native village, which by then had been absorbed by Russia with the westward shift in Poland's boundaries, or going to America. It wasn't an easy decision, but since no one in her family had survived the war and she had a cousin in St. Paul, she went to America. She was able to get a job as a nurse's aide at St. Joseph's Hospital while she learned English and worked on being recertified. She lived with her cousin on Magnolia Avenue and started attending St. Casimir on Geranium Avenue, only a few blocks away. The church sponsored a lot of social activities at which displaced persons like herself could meet members of the community.

It was at a dance, with a polka band, that Eva's mother met her father. Eva could never understand what they saw in each other, they were so different. Her mother was fair and solid, while her father was dark and gaunt. Her mother was positive, while her father was negative. Her mother was gregarious, while her father was solitary. Her mother was approachable, while her father was distant. Her mother looked to the future, while her father couldn't let go of the past. They were opposite in every way, but maybe that was the attraction. And they did have some major things in common: they were both Polish, they were both Catholic, they were both displaced persons, and they were both working at jobs beneath their qualifications because they didn't speak much English. There was also a physical attraction, which Eva didn't understand until she met Marek.

Within six months of the dance her father and mother were married in the church of St. Casimir, and within six weeks of the wedding her mother was pregnant. With their two incomes they were able to buy the house on Rose Avenue where they still lived, though it really hadn't been big enough for the three boys who followed Eva. But then no house would have been big enough for those boys.

From watching her parents Eva knew that her mother tried very hard to make her father happy but mostly in vain. Her father would occasionally smile, but it wasn't long before that look of ineffable sadness returned to his eyes.

One evening after dinner, while Eva was helping with the dishes, she asked her mother: "Why is Papa always sad?"

"He isn't always sad," her mother said, handing her a rinsed plate. As usual, her mother washed and Eva dried.

"Well, he always looks sad."

"No, he doesn't. He looks sad at times, but not always."

"Then why does he look sad at times?"

Her mother considered and then said: "Because he lost his home, he lost his family."

"But he has a home, and he has a family."

"I meant his home and his family in Poland."

"Where did he live in Poland?"

"In Warsaw."

"Did he live in a house?"

"He lived in a very nice house."

"What happened to it?"

"The Germans bombed it."

"Was his family inside it?"

"His mother and his grandmother were."

"What about his father?"

"The Germans shot his father," her mother said, "and they shot his brothers."

"How many brothers did he have?"

"Two. He also had a sister."

"What happened to her?"

Her mother paused for a long time and finally said: "The Germans killed her."

"Did the Germans kill your family too?"

"No. The Russians killed them."

"So why aren't you sad?"

"When I think about them I *am* sad."

"But you don't think about them all the time."

"I'm too busy to think about them. And I have you, your father, and your brothers to think about," her mother added, handing her another plate.

"So does Papa think about his family in Poland more than he thinks about us?"

"No. But he thinks about Poland more than I do."

She dried the plate and put it back into the cupboard where it belonged. "I wish I could make Papa happy."

"You do make him happy."

"I don't feel like I do. I feel like I can't do anything to make him happy."

"Believe me, you make him happy every time he sees you."

"He doesn't show it."

"Some people don't show how they feel."

"Why don't they?"

"That's just how they are."

"But when he doesn't show me how he feels, it makes me wonder about my own feeling."

"You mean you wonder if you really love him?"

"Sometimes I do. And then I feel bad."

"You shouldn't feel bad, and you shouldn't question your own feeling just because he doesn't respond to it. You love him, pure and simple. But don't ever think that by loving someone you can make him happy."

"If you can't, then what's the good of loving someone?"

"It lets God into your heart."

"How does it do that?"

"God is love," her mother said, "and love is God. So when you love someone, God is in your heart."

"If love is God, then you should be able to make a person happy by loving him."

"Being loved can't make you happy. Only loving can make you happy."

"Being loved by you makes me happy."

"No, it doesn't. Loving me is what makes you happy."

"But if you love someone enough," she argued, "you should be able to make him happy."

"You can't love anyone enough to make him happy. Only God can do that."

She tried to accept this, but she wondered if her mother was trying to justify the fact that she didn't love her father enough to make him happy.

The church had a school, which she attended from kindergarten through eighth grade. She liked the school for three main reasons: the teachers were mostly nuns, there were no boys, and she could walk there.

Her favorite nun was Sister Urszula, who taught her section of fifth grade and became her role model. It was Urszula who started her thinking about what she would do with her life, and of course one possibility was becoming a nun. But Urszula expanded the list to teaching and nursing, both of which professions you could practice as a nun, though you didn't have to be a nun. And it was Urszula who introduced her to St. Thérèse of Lisieux.

It happened during the year when they were preparing for their confirmation, and for Eva it solved the problem of finding a name. Her given name was Ewa Maria Koziol, but in second grade she had changed the spelling of her first name so that people who didn't know how to pronounce Polish wouldn't call her Ewe-a. She liked the name Maria, and she would have taken it for a confirmation name if she didn't already have it. So she was at a loss for a name until Urszula gave her a little book called *The Story of a Soul.*

The book gave her a mission in life. She knew from listening to her father and his colleagues that she couldn't do what they talked about—change the world by liberating Poland from the Russians. Men could do that kind of thing, or maybe they couldn't. Maybe they could only talk about it. And what if you had to kill people to achieve your mission? Did any mission justify killing people? Wasn't there another way?

Thérèse showed her another way, the "Little Way." Instead of performing heroic acts, you could express your love of God by doing little things. "Love proves itself by deeds," Thérèse wrote, "so how am I to show my love? Great deeds are forbidden me. The only way I can prove my love is by scattering flowers and these flowers are every little sacrifice, every glance and word, and the doing of the least actions for love."

The book answered all the questions Eva had raised with her mother. You could help people by little acts of love. You could even make them happy. But your love had to be unconditional. It couldn't depend on people loving you in return. And you didn't need that. You already had enough love from God to sustain you no matter what happened.

Declaring her mission, Thérèse said: "I will spend my heaven doing good on earth. I will let fall a shower of roses."

She took Thérèse as her confirmation name and tried to emulate her in everything she did. In particular, she did little things for her father without expecting anything in return. She loved her father unconditionally.

Three days later Marek returned to Poland, leaving her alone again. She wished he could have waited until Friday since Juliana was giving a concert on Thursday at Wigmore Hall, and she would have liked her husband to see her friend perform. At least Wigmore was only a short walk from where they lived, and Adrian met her in the lobby and sat with her. He had tickets in the third row, in a location where you could see Juliana's hands on the keyboard of her harpsichord.

Eva had no education in music, and she had never attended a concert in classical music. Except for Chopin, she knew the composers only by name: Bach, Beethoven, Brahms, Schubert, and a few others. She couldn't have identified their music. She had heard Chopin because her father had some records that he played on patriotic occasions, but that was it. And of course she had never heard anyone play a harpsichord.

According to the program, Juliana was going to play music by Bach—partitas and suites in the first half, and *The Italian Concerto* in the second half. As she waited for the concert to begin, she watched Juliana tuning her instrument. Adrian explained that you brought your own harpsichord to the concert hall, just as you brought your own violin.

She liked Adrian, a tall handsome Englishman with blond hair and blue eyes, which he attributed to Viking ancestors. Juliana had met him while he was working in Rio at the law firm that his firm used for Brazilian loans. He had spent two years there during the boom in bank lending to Brazil so that he could be more useful to his firm's clients. Though the boom was over and the firm's clients were restructuring loans, his experience was still useful, and he had more than enough to do, though unlike Marek he balanced his work life and his personal life.

Juliana had recently returned to Rio after two years in New York, where she had lived with a family headed by a man who had gone to medical school with her father. Though her father could have easily afforded to pay the rent on an apartment for her, he wanted her under some kind of family supervision, not wanting his nineteen-year-old daughter on her own in New York. But she had enjoyed some freedom in New York, and coming home to live with her family was a regression not only in her personal development but also in her professional development. After New York, Rio seemed like a cultural desert. There were few concerts for her to go to, and no opportunities for her to perform. Of course her parents, who expected her to get married and have children and play music only for her own enjoyment, didn't worry about her professional development. They worried about her getting involved in politics again.

Falling in love with Adrian, whom she met at an embassy party, enabled her to do what her parents wanted for her as well as what she wanted for herself. She was married, she was safe in London, she was planning to have children, and she was pursuing a musical career, performing tonight at Wigmore Hall.

Eva applauded with the rest of the audience when her friend came out, bowed, and sat down at her harpsichord. She listened attentively, and right away she could tell the difference between Bach and Chopin: Chopin's music came from passion, whereas Bach's music came from faith.

At the end of the final piece in the first half, French Suite V in G major, Juliana played what sounded like an Irish dance, except that instead of bodies dancing, it was souls dancing. And it was the most exhilarating music that Eva had heard. It literally took her breath away.

When it was over she had to remind herself to applaud, and when she did, she rose to her feet along with the rest of the audience, who shouted: "Bravo! Bravo!"

During the break Adrian bought two glasses of champagne, which they drank in a toast to Juliana.

"I'm so happy for her," Adrian said with a light in his eyes. "She worked so hard to get here."

"I'm seeing a whole different side of her," Eva said.

"Oh, music is another world. I can appreciate it, but I can't go where she goes when she's playing."

They returned to their seats for the second half and settled down. *The Italian Concerto* was a different kind of piece. It began with a fast assertive movement, and then went into a slow contemplative movement, which revealed Bach's compassion for people who have lost something, and then it ended with a very fast joyful movement. Listening to this music, Eva felt that it could have been composed only by someone who had known God. And she made a decision to hear more of Bach's music, especially his religious music.

When they met Juliana after the concert, Adrian gave her a hug that lifted her off the ground.

"*Você estava maravilhosa!*" he told her.

"*Obrigado, meu amor,*" Juliana said.

Eva had the feeling that her husband's compliment meant more to Juliana than all the applause.

"How did you like it?" Juliana asked her.

"*To transportowane mnie,*" she said instinctively.

"What does that mean?"

"It transported me. But I think it sounds better in Polish."

"I'm glad it did something for you," Juliana said, taking her hand. "*Estou tão feliz.*"

Marek was in Poland for Easter, but it didn't matter since he wouldn't have gone to church with her. In his mind Easter was a pagan feast day that the Christians had taken over.

The next day her course started. She took the tube from Baker Street to King's Cross, where she changed to the Piccadilly Line and continued to Russell Square.

As usual, she was disoriented when she emerged from the tube, but with the help of a young man who looked like a student she found the right building.

She was early, and the classroom was empty when she walked in. Not sure it was the right room, she refrained from taking a seat until another person came through the door. It was a man who had salt and pepper hair and twinkling blue eyes. He was tall and lean, and he looked like a model in his dark gray suit. The real surprise was the clerical collar.

"Is this the room for Adult Development?" she asked him.

"I hope it is," he said in what sounded like an Oxbridge accent. "That's what I'm here for."

"You're not the professor?"

"Oh, no. I'm just another student. My name is Francis," he said, extending his hand.

"Father Francis?"

"Yes, but you can call me Francis."

"I'm Eva," she said, shaking his hand. "Are you Anglican?"

"No. I'm Roman Catholic. And don't ask me what I'm doing in a psychology course."

"I'm Catholic too. Are you a pastor?"

"I'm a counselor. I'm a substitute pastor when they need me, but mainly I do counseling."

"Is that why you're taking a psychology course?"

"Right," he said, smiling and showing unusually good teeth for an Englishman. When she had remarked on their bad teeth Juliana had told her it was because they ate so much sugar—the one thing they had in common with Brazilians.

"Well, since we're in the right room," she said, "I guess we can sit down."

"Yes. Where do you usually sit in a classroom?"

"I usually sit in the front row."

"I'm sure the professor will like that," he said. "Do you mind if I sit next to you?"

"No, not at all. I need your support."

"You mean you've been out of school for a while?"

"It's only a year. But it seems like a long time."

"Well, I've been out of school for more than five years, so I need *your* support."

They sat down in the middle of the front row. They were still the only people in the room, so they kept talking.

"From your accent," Francis said, "I gather you're American."

"Yes. And I gather you're English."

"Actually, I'm Irish. But I've lived in England for five years. Since I was twenty-five," he added, revealing his age.

"I'm twenty-three," Eva said, reciprocating.

"Is your degree in psychology?"

"No. It's in nursing."

"You're a nurse? That's wonderful. What's your specialty?"

"Pediatrics," she said with professional pride.

"Then you must love children."

"I do," she said. "I wouldn't ever change my specialty. I'm only taking this course because I can't work until they approve my registration."

"I imagine it takes a long time."

"It does. And in the meantime I need something to do."

"There are other courses you could have taken."

"I guess I wanted to expand my horizons."

"That's why I'm taking the course."

A bearded man, wearing a black turtleneck, finally appeared. He looked around the room and asked: "Where are they?"

"You mean the other students?" Francis said. "How many are there supposed to be?"

"They told me twenty. I only count two."

"Well, we can make up for them."

"I'm sure you can, father."

The man began to take papers out of his briefcase.

Eva checked her watch. There were still five minutes before the class started.

During that time the man introduced himself and got their names. He was reviewing his lecture notes when the other students filed in. It was as if they had been lined up somewhere waiting for the minute hand of the clock to touch the hour.

When the class was over Eva shared a taxi with Francis, who was going in the same direction. She insisted on splitting the cost with him, and she pressed a note into his hand as she got out at Baker Street.

If she had been in New York she would have stopped at a deli and gotten a salad, but she didn't have that option in London. And she couldn't go into a pub alone. So she walked home, wondering what she had in the refrigerator.

She was looking for something to eat when the phone rang.

"Hello?" she said cautiously.

"It's me," Marek said.

She thanked God. "Are you all right?"

"Yes. I'm fine. I called you earlier, but you didn't answer."

"I was at my class. It started this evening."

"How did it go?"

"It was interesting," she said. "I like the professor, though he's a little weird."

"Well, he's a psychologist. What did you expect?" Marek had no more use for psychology than he did for religion.

"I met a nice priest in the class."

"I never met a nice priest."

"What about the one who married us?"

"Oh, he was all right. At least he didn't hit me." Marek claimed that a priest in elementary school had disciplined him by whacking him on the back of the head, and that it had hurt the priest's hand more than it had hurt Marek.

She had no trouble imagining him as a little boy who defied authority. "How much longer will you have to stay there?"

"A few more days. We have some meetings about the budget." He couldn't make any reference to what he was really doing in Poland since their conversation was undoubtedly being recorded by the secret police.

"That sounds like fun. Where did you have dinner tonight?"

"In the hotel restaurant."

"Has it gotten any better?"

"No. I think it's gotten worse."

"Then why don't you eat somewhere else?"

"I don't have a lot of choices. It's not like New York."

"It's not like New York here either. On the way home from class I would have liked to stop at a deli and get a salad, but there was nothing open."

"The pubs were open." Of course he was joking. He wouldn't have wanted her to go into a pub alone.

"You can't get a takeout salad at a pub."

"How do you know? You never tried. And in London they call it a takeaway."

She wondered how he learned such things when he was almost never in London. "I'll try to remember that next time I go into a pub."

"So you have nothing to eat tonight?"

"I was looking for something when you called."

"Well, the food was so bad in the restaurant that I would have done better not to eat."

"I guess I'd do better not to eat. I need to lose weight."

"You don't need to lose weight. You're absolutely perfect."

That made her feel good. She knew he wasn't just saying it, he really meant it. "I wish you were here. I really miss you."

"I miss you too."

"Come home as soon as you can."

"I will."

When they had hung up she went into the kitchen and poured herself a glass of brandy and then returned to the living room, where she sank into the sofa. She sipped the brandy, recalling how they had made love on the sofa only a week ago.

She was longing for him when the phone rang again.

Assuming it was Marek, who must have forgotten to tell her something, she jumped up and rushed to the phone.

She was so certain it was her husband—there was no one in London who might be calling her, other than Juliana, who never called her in the evening—that instead of saying hello, she said in Polish: "I'm having a glass of brandy for dinner."

"Oh, I'm sorry," a woman said in Polish. "I must have the wrong number."

If she hadn't answered the phone in Polish and the woman hadn't responded in Polish, she would have believed that the woman did have the wrong number. But her suspicions were aroused. "Who were you calling?"

"Marek Ostrowski."

"Then you have the right number."

"I do? Well—" The woman evidently didn't know what to say. But she didn't hang up, she stayed on the phone as if she were waiting for something.

The woman had a young voice, so Eva thought she might be a student in exile working with Lukasz and Czeslaw. "Are you calling for Lukasz?"

"No. I was calling—" The woman stopped.

"Would you like to leave a message?"

"No. I'm sorry," the woman said before hanging up.

Eva stood holding the phone and wondering. If this young woman knew Marek she would know he was away. If she didn't know him why had she called? Was she trying to meet him? Had she just arrived from Poland and been given Marek's name as someone to contact? But then why hadn't she left a message?

It didn't make sense.

THREE

THE SOCIAL LIFE of Eva's parents centered around the church and the Polish-American Club on Arcade Street, where almost every weekend there was a family event. The biggest event at the club was Pulaski Day, when they had a live polka band along with the usual Polish food and local beer. On a typical Saturday night they danced to the records of famous polka bands like Whoopee John and Jolly Stan.

Eva learned to dance from her mother, who taught her the polka, the waltz, and the foxtrot. Until she was fourteen, her mother and her father were the only people she had ever danced with. According to the people who watched them, her mother and her father were good dancers, but her father always had to be talked into dancing. He preferred to stand on the sidelines, smoking cigarettes and drinking vodka as he watched the other people dance. But her mother could coax him out onto the floor for a slow waltz.

Occasionally, he would agree to dance the polka with Eva. Of course she always had to ask him to dance, just as her mother did. But as they whirled around the floor together, she would see a flicker of joy in his eyes, and she would be glad. As far as she could tell, it was the closest she came to making him happy.

Meanwhile, outside of this community people her age (she was twelve at the time) were listening to the music of the Beatles and the Rolling Stones and Jimi Hendrix and Janis Joplin. They didn't play that kind of music at the Polish-American Club. About the only pop music they played were the love songs of Bobby Vinton, the Polish Prince, such as "Roses are Red (My Love)" and "Blue Velvet" and "There! I've Said It Again." The older people never got tired of playing those songs, not only because they were good songs but also because Bobby Vinton (Vintula) was one of them, a Polish-American who had become a star. The younger people were tired of hearing him, and one evening a boy in high school smuggled some of his records into the club, and while the man who played the role of disk jockey wasn't watching, he slipped in a record of "I Can't Get No Satisfaction" by the Rolling Stones.

It was like flaunting a book from the condemned list, and the older people were as shocked as the younger people were excited. The boy who had put on the record started to dance with the girl he was with, but they didn't get far. The disk jockey lifted the arm off the record and stopped the music. A few of the younger people booed, but most of them were resigned to this act of censure. Unlike the university students who at that time were protesting in Spain and Germany and Czechoslovakia and Mexico and of course Poland, where at the moment they were battling the police in the streets of Warsaw, most of these young people weren't confrontational. They had been raised strictly in a tight community bounded by St. Casimir, the Polish-American Club, and the Catholic schools they attended, and few of them were ready to rebel. So most of them resumed dancing to the approved music of Bobby Vinton.

By her freshman year in high school Eva had begun to acquire a different perspective. She became aware of this change in her view one Saturday night at the club when a boy she had known since kindergarten asked her to dance to "Blue Velvet." She was standing on the sidelines next to her mother, who gave her a nudge in the middle of her back when it looked as if Eva was going to turn the boy down.

His name was Stanley, and he was a big blond boy, a foot and a half taller than she was, and she had never been attracted to him. Now, with her mother's insistent fingers poking at her back, she realized that she was sick of "Blue Velvet" and that Stanley was the last person in the world she wanted to dance with.

But before she could turn him down he grabbed her right hand and put his arm around her waist and dragged her out onto the floor. Since everyone was watching, she had to make the best of it, but she resisted Stanley's efforts to draw her close to him. With gritted teeth she stared ahead at what was already beginning to look like a beer belly and went through the motions of dancing. She thanked God when the song ended and quickly released herself from Stanley and stomped back to her mother, saying: "I want to go home."

"We're not ready to leave yet," her mother said.

"Well, I can go home by myself."

"I don't want you walking alone at night."

"Nothing could happen that would be any worse than what just did happen."

Her mother looked at her with concern. "We need to talk."

"We can't talk here."

"Then let's go into the lounge."

She followed her mother out of the hall and into the lounge, where they sat down in a corner.

As they talked, the women who passed through the lounge going into and coming out of the bathroom respected their privacy.

"What's the problem?" her mother asked gently.

"I didn't want to dance with that boy."

"Why not?"

"I don't like him."

"Why don't you like him?"

"I don't know. I just don't like him."

"It's the first time I heard you say you don't like him. You've known him all your life."

"Well, maybe that's the problem. Maybe I'm sick of him, just like I'm sick of Bobby Vinton and sick of Polacks."

Her mother smiled. "Polacks?"

"I'm sorry. I wasn't making an ethnic slur."

"It sounded like you were. Remember, you're a Polack."

"I know. But sometimes I wish I wasn't Polish. Sometimes I wish I had a normal name."

"A normal name? Like Mary Smith?"

"At least a name that people could pronounce."

"You're lucky," her mother said with a laugh. "Your last name could have been Wojciechowski."

"It could have been Anderson or Johnson." A lot of Swedes lived on the east side of St. Paul, so if you were Swedish you might feel like you belonged to the majority.

"Well, you can wish you weren't Polish, but you *are* Polish. That's your heritage. And you should be proud of it."

"I'm proud of it, but I'm sick of hearing about Kościuszko and Pulaski."

"I understand. But you're not stuck in this neighborhood. You speak English the way your father and I will never be able to speak it."

"Is that why you live here?"

"We feel at home here."

"But I don't want to stay here."

"I don't want you to stay here. I want you to get out of here. I mean, I don't want you to go so far away that I won't see you. But I do want you to get out of here."

"Then why did you push me into dancing with that boy?"

"I guess I was acting out of instinct."

"You mean deep down you want me to marry a Polish man?"

"I guess I do," her mother admitted. "I want you to marry someone who has the same background."

Eva wondered. "What if I fell in love with someone who had a different background?"

"Falling in love with someone is one thing. Marrying him is another thing."

"You fell in love with Papa, didn't you?"

"Oh, yes. I fell in love with him. But I wouldn't have married him if we hadn't had a lot of things in common."

"Like being Polish?"

"Like having the same values."

She pondered this. "Well, couldn't you have the same values as someone who had a different background?"

"I suppose you could. But when you meet someone, you don't know what his values are. It takes a while to discover what someone's values are."

"So if he has the same background, he has the same values?"

"Not necessarily. But if he has the same background, you know something about him."

"What do you know?"

"You know how he's been raised."

"He could have been raised to be a good person," Eva argued, "and turn out bad."

"You're right. There isn't any guarantee. But parents feel safer if their children marry people who have the same background."

"What if I didn't marry anyone?"

"What do you mean?"

"I could become a nun."

"Are you still seriously considering that?"

"I don't know. I just can't imagine being married."

"You don't have to imagine it. You're only fourteen. So how did we get on the subject of marriage?"

"I brought it up. I asked why you pushed me into dancing with that boy."

"So now you know why. But I promise not to do that again."

"Thanks, Mom. And I promise not to rule out marrying a Polish man. But I don't think I will," she added, sure of herself.

During the summer before her senior year in high school Eva worked as an aide at St. Joseph's Hospital. When she started the job she hadn't decided to be a nurse, though she had decided not to be a nun—which still left the possibility of being a teacher.

Her work at the hospital involved doing all the little things that had to be done but no one wanted to do, such as changing soiled sheets and emptying bedpans. In a way it was like the work her mother did at home, and it gave Eva a deeper appreciation of her mother. It also made her feel that she was following the path of St. Thérèse by making little daily sacrifices instead of performing great deeds, as the doctors did.

Her commitment to nursing began in July when she walked into the room of a new patient whose last name was Maciejewski. The patient was an old woman who had lost so much weight that her face was like a skull with a thin almost translucent layer of skin on it. She was dying of cancer and was in a lot of pain, but a light was still shining from the deep sockets of her eyes, and when she saw Eva's last name on her uniform she eagerly asked: "*Mówisz po polsku?*"

"Yes, I speak Polish," Eva said, stopping at the bedside.

"That's wonderful. I don't speak English, and no one in this hospital can understand me, except one nurse. Her name is Koziol. Are you related to her?"

"She's my mother."

"Are you a nurse too?"

"No. I'm not. I'm only an aide."

"Are you going to follow in your mother's footsteps?"

"I'm not sure. I'm thinking about it."

"Don't think about it. Just do it. You couldn't have a better profession. And you couldn't have a better role model than your mother."

"She's a very good nurse," Eva agreed.

"She's more than a nurse. Your mother's a saint."

She hadn't ever thought of her mother as a saint, and she was humbled by the possibility that she had undervalued her mother.

"Did you go to a Catholic school?" the old woman asked.

"Yes. I went to St. Casimir, and then to St. Bernard, and now I'm in the nursing program at St. Catherine."

"Then you must have read about the saints."

"We read about their lives in elementary school."

"What's your patron saint?"

"It's Saint Thérèse of Lisieux."

"St. Thérèse of Lisieux," the old woman repeated. "Now, that tells me something about you."

"What does it tell you?"

"It tells me you'd be a very good nurse."

"Then you must know her book."

"I read it many years ago. I'd love to read it again, but my eyes are so bad I can't read anything."

"I could read it to you. I mean, after I'm off work."

"You'd do that for me?" the old woman said as if she were deeply touched.

"Of course I would." It had occurred to Eva that this old woman could have been her *babcia*, her father's mother who had been killed by the Germans or her mother's mother who had been killed by the Russians.

"Do you have it in Polish?"

"I have it in English, but I could get a Polish version."

"It must be wonderful to know both languages."

"Well, I was born here. For me it was easy."

"I was born in Białystok. Do you know where that is?"

"It's in the northeast of Poland, near the border with Russia."

The old woman nodded. "That's right. You must have studied the geography of Poland."

"I went to a Polish school," she explained.

"Your mother told me she was from Poland, from a village that's now in Russia."

"My father's from Poland too. They were displaced persons."

"Displaced persons. That's an apt description."

"Did you come here after the war?"

"I came here with my daughter and her two children. She lost her husband to the Russians. She got a job as a cleaning woman at the Seeger plant while I looked after her children. She had a degree in chemistry."

"Did she eventually get a better job?"

"No. She died of cancer when she was twenty-seven."

"I'm sorry," Eva said with genuine sympathy.

After a silence the old woman said: "She left me with two wonderful grandchildren."

"Did you raise them?"

"I did. Don't ask me what we lived on. But we never went on welfare."

"How old are they now?"

"The girl is thirty-two. She lives in Minneapolis, and she has three children. The boy is thirty. He lives in Chicago. He's an engineer."

"I assume they come and visit you."

"The girl does. She brought me here. She comes and visits me almost every day. The boy— Well, you know how boys are. He'll come for my funeral."

She did know how boys were, and so far she hadn't found any use for them.

"Well, I've enjoyed talking with you," the old woman said as if she were conscious of the fact that Eva was supposed to be working.

Eva made sure that the old woman was comfortable, and then she checked to see if the other patient in the room needed anything. The other patient, a young woman recovering from an appendectomy, was fast asleep.

On the way home she stopped at the elementary school and found Sister Urszula, who had a Polish version of the book and happily loaned it to her.

The next day after four, when she was off, she went to Mrs. Maciejewski's room and stayed there for a while, sitting in a chair and reading aloud from *The Story of a Soul*. She had never read it in Polish, and maybe for that reason she found new meaning in what Thérèse had written.

"I have always wanted to become a saint," Eva read. "Unfortunately when I have compared myself with the saints, I have always found that there is the same difference between the saints and me as there is between a mountain whose summit is lost in the clouds and a humble grain of sand trodden underfoot by passers-by. Instead of being discouraged, I told myself: God would not make me wish for something impossible and so, in spite of my littleness, I can aim at being a saint. It is impossible for me to grow bigger, so I put up with myself as I am, with all my countless faults. But I will look for some means of going to heaven by a little way which is very short and very straight, a little way that is quite new."

"You read that well," the old woman told her.

"Thank you," she said, blushing from the compliment.

"I can tell that you identify with her."

"Well, I'm little like her."

"How tall are you?"

"Five feet one."

"That's tall enough."

"You mean for a girl."

"I mean for anyone. My husband was only five feet four. But that was tall enough."

"My father's over six feet, and my brothers are already taller than I am."

"How many brothers do you have?"

"I have three brothers."

"You make it sound like three too many."

"Well, they're not good for anything."

"You shouldn't judge them. They're only boys."

"But why should they have special dispensation?"

"Because they need it. Boys aren't as strong as girls."

"They're stronger physically."

"That's all. And when they're wrong, they always resort to physical force."

"But why don't they just admit they're wrong?"

"It's hard for them to admit they're wrong."

"Is that why the Russians won't leave Poland? Because it's hard for them to admit they were wrong to take it over?"

"They think they were right to take over Poland."

"But why did they take it over?" Eva asked. "I've listened to my father and his friends talk about it, over and over, but I still don't understand it."

"The Russians want to control Poland."

"So the Russians are like the boys at school who are always interfering with other people?"

"They have the same motive as those boys. They want to control other people."

"They hurt people, they kill people just to control them?"

"To control them and have power over them."

"Well, if men are like that," Eva said, "then they shouldn't be running the world."

"All men aren't like that, and some women are like that. So let's say that people like that shouldn't be running the world."

"But they *are* running the world."

"They are. And as long as they are, we have to stop them from destroying it."

"How can we do that?"

"The way your patron saint told us—by doing the little things that make the world a better place."

"I don't think the feminists would agree with that."

"You mean those women who say that women should be more like men? But that would only make things worse. The way to make things better is for men to be more like women. That's what the feminists should be saying."

At that moment a doctor in a khaki suit breezed into the room and stopped at the side of the bed and asked the patient: "How are you doing?"

"I'm doing fine," Mrs. Maciejewski said in broken English.

"Is the medicine helping?"

The old woman appealed to Eva, who translated this question for her.

"Tell the doctor I'm feeling less pain."

Eva translated that for the doctor.

"You speak Polish?" the doctor said, surprised. "You don't look Polish. You look Italian."

"I'm Polish," she said. "A hundred percent."

In her senior year at high school Eva got straight A's, and she was admitted to the nursing program at St. Catherine College, which gave her a scholarship. By then she knew what she wanted to do, and she sailed through the program doing her clinical work at Children's Hospital and envisioning a career there.

She planned to move out of her parents' house when she got a job and found a colleague to share an apartment with. She couldn't wait to get away from her brothers, who seemed to occupy the whole house. Two of them were in high school now and playing football, while the third was in middle school but was already a head taller than she was. When she saw them together in the living room, watching a Minnesota Vikings game, she couldn't help thinking that they were exactly the type of boy she would never marry. They reminded her of Stanley, the boy who had made her dance with him that night at the Polish-American Club, and though she had promised not to rule out marrying a Polish man, she couldn't imagine doing it.

Then something happened that caused her to alter her plans. She was downtown shopping one afternoon in April when she saw a man and a woman going into a hotel. It wasn't the St. Paul Hotel but one of those nameless hotels with a red neon light that said "Hotel" and another light that said "Vacancy." The man was her father, and the woman wasn't her mother.

She stopped and stared as the door closed behind them, feeling like she was going to throw up. She wanted to believe that they were just going into the hotel to have a cup of coffee or a bite to eat, but the hotel didn't have a sign for a restaurant. It was the kind of place that only had beds.

For a while she stood there wondering if she should wait until they came out, and she tried to imagine what would happen.

"What were you doing with that woman?" she would ask.

"This isn't what it looks like," her father would say.

"Then what is it?"

"It's nothing, nothing."

She couldn't stomach the thought of having such a sordid scene. She could confront him later and tell him she had seen him go into a hotel with a woman. But if she didn't catch him in the act, then he could deny it. And she couldn't ever prove it.

Or maybe he wouldn't deny it. Maybe he would tell her that he no longer loved her mother, and that they were going to get a divorce. Maybe he would try to justify what he had done.

After playing through a number of scenes she realized that she didn't want to hear what her father had to say. Whatever he said, it would only make things worse.

So should she tell her mother?

She could easily imagine how her mother would feel, and she knew she couldn't tell her mother something that would hurt so much. The affair might be nothing, as she had imagined her father arguing, so what good could possibly come from telling her mother?

But if she didn't tell her mother, she would be deceiving her, just as her father was deceiving her. She would be living a lie with her mother. But it would only hurt *her* to live a lie. It wouldn't hurt her mother.

Finally, she at least decided not to stay there until her father and the woman came out of the hotel.

On the way home she stopped at St. Casimir and prayed for guidance. She came away with the resolution not to do anything that would hurt her mother. That meant not telling her mother as well as not confronting her father.

After sitting through dinner with her parents at opposite ends of the table and her brothers on both sides, she realized that she not only had to get out of the house, but she also had to get out of St. Paul. She couldn't face her parents knowing what had happened and pretending she didn't know.

The next day she went to the placement office of the college and learned that New York Hospital had an opening for a pediatric nurse. The information had come from a doctor named Bridget Ryan, who was a graduate of the St. Catherine nursing program and would presumably favor applicants from it.

Without hesitation Eva applied for the position, and she was assured that with the strong recommendations from the college, she was likely to get it.

Eva waited until the day after Marek returned from Poland to mention that an unidentified woman had called him. She had considered not mentioning it, but then she would have been withholding information from him, going against their principle of being completely honest with each other. It also might have indicated that she had something to worry about.

They were at the dinner table, eating pasta and drinking red Rhone wine when she brought it up, saying: "While you were away, someone called you."

"Who was it?" he asked, looking up from his plate.

"She wouldn't say. And she wouldn't leave a message."

"You mean it was a woman?"

"A young woman."

"Did she speak Polish?"

"Yes. She did."

"It's probably a student who escaped from Poland."

"That's what I figured," Eva said. "But how did she get your phone number?"

"She could have gotten my number from Lukasz. If she needed help, he would have told her to contact me. The students all come to me for help."

"If she needed help, then why wouldn't she leave a message?"

"She might have been afraid to leave one," Marek said as if he understood the young woman's behavior. "Or she might have had information for me."

"I hadn't thought of that," Eva admitted. The young woman might have been warned not to say anything over the phone that could fall into the wrong hands.

"Did you tell her when I'd be back?"

"No. I didn't know when you'd be back. And she didn't ask. She just hung up."

"Well, she'll probably call again." He casually reached for the bottle of wine and poured himself some more. "I'll ask Lukasz about her. They're coming tomorrow night for dinner. They're bringing the food, so you don't have to cook."

"What are they bringing? Chinese food?"

"No. Polish food. I don't know where they're getting it. But I know they're not cooking it themselves."

The next evening she could smell the *kielbasa* as they were coming up the stairs. They had bags of food, not only the *kielbasa* but also *pierogi* and sauerkraut and potato pancakes and stuffed cabbage.

"We have two kinds of *pierogi*," Czeslaw told her. "Cheese and mushroom."

"Where did you get all this? From a Polish takeaway?"

"From a woman in our building. We helped her move some furniture, and this was her way of repaying us."

"She should open a restaurant," Lukasz said. "With all the Polish people in London, there must be a market for Polish food."

They took the food into the kitchen, where Marek got out the bottle of vodka and poured them shots. They began the meeting as usual with a hearty "*Na zdrowie!*"

Then Marek reported what he had learned in Poland. Jaruzelski was proceeding with his plan for a military takeover, operating on the assumption that Russia would finally agree to support him by sending in troops. He had set a date in October for implementing this plan, which included massive arrests of union leaders, student leaders, political leaders, and anyone else who might oppose the dictatorship.

"It'll be like Chile or Argentina," Marek told them.

"They all went to the same school," Lukasz said, meaning the military.

"It makes no difference if they're communists or fascists," Czeslaw agreed. "The military are all the same. They all want power."

"But they don't know what to do with it," Marek said. "So they end up abusing it."

"If Russia supports him, how the hell are we going to stop him?" Lukasz asked.

"I think he's operating on a false assumption."

"What do you mean?"

"I don't think Russia will send in troops."

"Why don't you think so?"

"I have a source of information that says they won't. Now, it could be wrong, but it's worth betting on. If we do nothing," Marek said, "because we assume that Russia will send in troops, then Jaruzelski won't need them to implement his plan. But if we're prepared to counteract him, and if my source is right about Russia, then we can stop him."

"To stop him," Czeslaw pointed out, "we'll need an army."

"Yes. We will," Marek agreed.

"But that goes against the principle of nonviolence."

"There's a limit to that principle."

"I know. And there's the just war doctrine that permits violence under certain conditions. But I don't know if we have those conditions."

"We've been attacked," Marek argued. "Our response would be proportionate to the attack. We wouldn't harm civilians. And we have a reasonable chance of success."

Eva was impressed by how well Marek applied the criteria of the doctrine for a just war. At least he remembered something from his Catholic education.

"What do the leaders of Solidarity think about that?" Lukasz asked after a moment of reflection.

"They're still committed to nonviolence. But at the next level down some of them are open to the idea. And we could work with them."

"I want to make sure I understand what you're saying," Czeslaw said. "You're saying that we should build an army to counteract Jaruzelski."

"That's what I'm saying."

"What happened to the ten million people in the streets?"

"They'll still be there. But we have to stop Jaruzelski from arresting our leaders. If he does, then the ten million people won't have any direction."

"They'll have power," Lukasz said.

"But they won't know what to do with it."

"So our objective is to build an army that can stop Jaruzelski from arresting our leaders?"

Marek nodded. "That's right."

"How big an army do we need?"

"About two thousand well-armed, well-trained people."

"Only two thousand? Is that enough?"

"By historical standards, it's more than enough."

"Does the CIA support this plan?" Czeslaw asked.

"Of course they support it. All the way."

"Will they give us the money to buy arms?"

"Don't worry about the money. That won't be a problem. The problem," Marek said, "will be informers. If Jaruzelski finds out what we're doing, he'll intervene. And it'll get nasty."

"It's already nasty."

"Well, it'll get nastier."

As she laid the platters of Polish food on the table Eva was reminded of the feasts with her family in the house on Rose Avenue. It looked like there was more food than even her three brothers could handle. But Lukasz and Czeslaw, who were smaller than her brothers, cleaned the platters. As usual, she was amazed by their capacity.

While they were drinking brandy she went to the window, and she saw the two men who had been there last time watching the house. They stood in the shadows, so she couldn't see their faces, but she was sure it was the same two men.

Later, as she and Marek were lying in bed, she asked him if Lukasz had been able to tell him anything about the woman who had called.

"He said he didn't know who it could be," Marek told her.

"Then he didn't give her your phone number?"

"Evidently not."

"Then how did she get it?"

"I don't know. She could have gotten it from someone else. They all know me."

She had an idea, which eliminated one source of anxiety but created another. "Do you think she could be an informer?"

"She could be. They're here in London."

"I meant to tell you. The last time the boys came for dinner I saw two men standing on the street, watching the house. And they were there again tonight."

"You should have told me before."

"Well, I didn't want to be paranoid. I mean, they could have had a lot of reasons for standing there. But now I see a pattern. It happens when the boys come for dinner."

"They must be following them. I'll warn them."

She lay there alone while he got up and made a phone call. She could hear him speaking in Polish, using a code that she didn't understand. And she was glad she had told him about the two men. She really cared about those boys. She loved them more than her own brothers.

Marek was in Poland when a Turkish gunman fired four shots into the pope as he was passing through St. Peter's Square. The gunman was captured by a nun and some other people standing nearby, and the pope was rushed to a hospital with wounds in his left hand, his right arm, and his lower intestine. He lost so much blood that he was in critical condition, and Eva was among the many people who prayed for him. When she heard that he was going to survive she went to the Lady Chapel and thanked the Blessed Mother.

During this time Marek got through to her by phone, but they couldn't talk about what had happened. She had to wait for his return to hear his explanation. According to him, the plot had been hatched in Moscow, and the KGB had arranged through the Bulgarian Secret Service to hire the assassin. The motive was obvious. The pope supported Solidarity, which threatened the Russian empire, so he had to be eliminated.

"That's what I told Lukasz and Czeslaw at our last meeting," Marek reminded her. "The Russians can stop us if they eliminate our leaders."

"So you were right."

He nodded. "Yes. I just didn't think they'd start at the top. But now that they've started, all our leaders are in danger."

"What about you?"

"I'm not a leader. They don't even know who I am."

"They know you're a banker who travels regularly to Poland. Are you sure they don't know what you're doing?"

"I don't think they do. If they did, they wouldn't let me come and go so freely."

Eva was momentarily reassured, but then she remembered the phone call from that woman and the two men who watched the house when Lukasz and Czeslaw came for dinner. And she had no doubt that her husband was on their list.

FOUR

AFTER HER INTERVIEW with the nurse manager she was
scheduled to meet with Bridget Ryan, the doctor who had told
her college about the job opportunity. Dr. Ryan had an office on
the pediatrics floor of the hospital.

She was ushered into the doctor's office by a woman her
mother's age, who closed the door behind her.

The doctor was sitting behind a desk that had a pile of folders
on it, one of them open.

"Come on in," the doctor said, encouraging her with a
motion of her hand. She had short reddish hair and acute green
eyes that peered over the gold rims of her tinted glasses. "I
assume you're Eva."

"Yes, doctor," Eva said, approaching the desk.

"You can call me Bridget. Please sit down."

Eva sat down, trying to imagine calling this woman Bridget.
Her eyes wandered over to a framed black-and-white photograph
on the wall that showed a young woman in a uniform like the
kind she remembered seeing in an old issue of *Life Magazine*.

"That's me," Bridget said, following her eyes. "It was taken in
Pearl Harbor a few weeks after the Battle of Midway. I was your
age then, or not much older."

Based on what she had learned from studying history, she
figured that Bridget was in her mid-fifties.

"You had strong recommendations from the college and
from both the hospitals where you worked, so I have no doubt
that you'll get the job. But I know what it's like to come from St.
Paul and move to New York, and I wonder if you have any
concerns."

"I do," she admitted. "I've never lived away from home."

"Are you close to your family?"

"I guess I am. But it was time for me to leave."

"I understand. Do you have a big family?"

"I have three brothers."

"Are you the oldest?"

"Yes. I am." She wondered how Bridget had guessed.

"Well, I had eight brothers and sisters," Bridget said. "And I was the oldest."

"Did you grow up in St. Paul?" Eva asked, beginning to feel comfortable with this woman.

"We lived on Crocus Hill in a house that wasn't big enough."

"I know what you mean. We lived on the East Side in a house that wasn't big enough."

"What does your father do for a living?"

"He works at the Whirlpool plant. It used to be Seeger."

"I know where that is. What about your mother?"

"She's a nurse. She works at St. Joseph's."

"I did my clinical work there."

"I worked there as an aide during the summer."

"Well, let me tell you about New York," Bridget said, leaning forward and clasping her hands. "Whatever their profession, the people who work in New York City believe they're the best in the world. They're in the big leagues, and people who work in other cities are only on the farm teams. But don't let these people put you down. Your education in the nursing program at St. Catherine is as good as any, and so is your clinical experience at Children's Hospital. In fact, it's one of the top five hospitals in the country for pediatrics."

Eva nodded, believing the doctor.

"So I know you'll be good professionally. Your challenges will be in your life outside the hospital, as I know from my own experience. And I want you to know that if you ever want to talk with someone, I'm here for you. I know you don't need another mother, and I won't presume to be one, but at times it's good to have someone you can talk with who won't tell you what you should do, who'll just listen."

"Thank you," Eva said appreciatively.

"Now, speaking of challenges," Bridget said with a knowing look, "the hardest thing about moving to New York is finding a place to live."

"I was going to ask about that."

"Where are you staying?"

"I'm at the YWCA."

"I stayed there when I first came to New York. I'm sure it hasn't changed."

"It's all right. But it's expensive."

"It's less than you'd pay at a decent hotel. But you might not have to stay there long. There's a nurse in our department who needs a roommate. Her name is Ramona, and she lives only a few blocks from here. It would be convenient."

"How do I contact her?"

"Find out what shift she's on and meet her on the floor."

"I mean, assuming I get the job."

"You'll get it. Don't worry," Bridget said as if she had already heard from the nurse manager and knew the decision.

She met Ramona that afternoon at the nursing desk, where they were introduced to each other by the manager on duty. By then she had been offered the job and accepted it, so she was ready to find a place to live.

Ramona had a serious face, with strong features and brown skin. She looked tough, but there was a playfulness in her eyes that made her less threatening.

"You're going to work here?" Ramona asked skeptically. "On this floor?"

"I start next week."

"Did they tell you I need a roommate?"

"Yes. You do, don't you?"

"It depends," Ramona said, assessing her. "I'm off at four. We could go and have a drink and see if we're compatible."

"Okay. Should I meet you here?"

"We can meet at a bar. It's called the Recovery Room. It's not far from the hospital. I'll tell you how to get there."

Eva had never been in a bar, except at the Polish-American Club in the company of her parents, and she had misgivings about going to a bar, but she took the directions from Ramona and arrived at the Recovery Room five minutes after the time they had agreed on, just to make sure she didn't get there first. She needn't have worried since she found Ramona already there, sitting at the bar with a half-empty glass in front of her.

"You made it," Ramona said as if she might have had some doubts. She picked up her glass. "Let's go to a booth."

"Okay," she said, following Ramona.

"What would you like to drink?"

"I don't know. What are you drinking?"

"A rum screwdriver," Ramona said as they sat down.

"What's that?"

"It's orange juice and rum. If you like orange juice, you'll like this drink."

"I like orange juice, but I've never had a drink before. I mean, except a taste of beer."

"You can have a beer if you want."

"No. I couldn't drink a whole bottle."

"Beer makes you pee."

"Well, maybe I should have the orange juice without the rum. I don't want to get the bar into trouble."

"How would you get the bar into trouble?"

"I'm only twenty."

"I am too," Ramona admitted.

"But isn't twenty-one the legal age for drinking?"

"Not in New York. It's eighteen. Where're you from?"

"I'm from Minnesota."

"I took geography in school, so I should know where that is, but I honestly don't."

"It's west of Chicago, west and north."

"Where's Chicago?" Ramona asked, deadpanning.

"It's west of New York," Eva said, catching on.

At that moment a young guy, who looked a few years older than they were, stopped at the booth and asked if he could get them anything.

"I'll have another rum screwdriver," Ramona told him.

"I'll have one too," Eva said, deciding to be adventurous.

"Two rum screwdrivers," the guy said after checking them out.

"His name is Tony," Ramona said when he had left them. "He wants to be an actor. All the waiters in New York want to be actors."

"Are you from New York?" Eva asked since Ramona seemed to know so much about the city.

"I was born and raised here, up in the Barrio."

"Where's that?"

"It's east of Minnesota."

Eva laughed.

"It's north of here, around 116th Street. It's a Puerto Rican neighborhood."

"Are you Puerto Rican?"

"Yeah. What're you?"

"I'm Polish."

"Really? I never met anyone Polish before. I know there're Polish people in the city, but they live in Brooklyn. And I've never been there."

"Do we have a lot of Puerto Rican patients?"

"Yeah. We also have a lot of Dominican patients."

"Then I need to learn Spanish."

"You can buy a book. And I'll teach you words that aren't in the book."

From this offer Eva inferred that Ramona had decided that they were compatible.

The waiter brought their drinks.

"It tastes like orange juice," Eva said after taking a sip.

"There's rum in it."

"I don't taste the rum."

"Well, that's the thing about rum. When you mix it with fruit, you don't taste it. But it's there, believe me."

After two drinks Eva believed her.

They were more than compatible as they walked from the bar to the street where Ramona lived. They entered an old tenement building that had fire escapes on the front of it, and they started climbing the three flights of stairs to Ramona's apartment.

"This will keep you in shape," Ramona said as they reached the landing on the second floor.

They paused to catch their breath and then continued.

The apartment was what they called a railroad flat. It ran from the front to the back of the building, and it had two bedrooms, a large kitchen, and a living room.

"It's two hundred and fifty a month," Ramona said.

"Two hundred and fifty?" The night before, Eva had looked in the *Times* classified section at apartments for rent, and they were more than eight hundred dollars for one bedroom.

"This apartment is under rent control. We can thank my previous roommate for that. She got the deal and passed it on."

"How much rent would you want from me?"

"We each pay half. I wouldn't try to make money off of you."

"Well, I appreciate it. You could have easily taken advantage of a hick from Minnesota."

"I don't take advantage of people," Ramona said seriously. "I've seen too much of that in my life. The word in Spanish is *aprovecharse.*"

Eva repeated the Spanish word, and Ramona corrected her pronunciation until she got it right.

They wandered into the kitchen, where Ramona said: "I have some food that my mother gave me. Would you like to try it?"

"Sure. I mean, if you have enough for both of us."

"I have enough food for a baseball team. My mother always worries that I'm not getting enough to eat, so she makes mountains of food for me."

"She sounds like my mother."

"Then watch out. Your mother might start sending you food from Minnesota."

As she watched Ramona take some plastic containers out of the refrigerator, she asked: "Where did you get your nursing degree?"

"At St. Catherine College."

"You're kidding me," Eva said, surprised.

"Why would I be kidding you?"

"I got my degree from St. Catherine College."

"There must be more than one St. Catherine College. I went to the one in Yonkers."

"I went to the one in St. Paul."

"Was it a Catholic college?"

"Oh, yes. I went to Catholic schools from the age of five."

"I did too. Then we must be tough. We both survived that experience."

"Do you go to church?"

"Almost every Sunday. I go to the noon mass, which usually gives me enough time to recover from whatever I did the night before."

"Where do you go?"

"St. Jean Baptiste. It's on Lexington at 76th Street. It's only a few blocks from here."

"I'm used to going earlier, but I could adjust to going later.'

"You'll want to go later. Believe me."

When Ramona had warmed up the food that her mother had given her, they sat down at the table in the kitchen and attacked it. There was fried chicken, white rice, pink beans, and fried plantains, which Eva knew the Spanish words for by the time they had finished.

As she drank the Puerto Rican coffee that Ramona had made, she felt that they had gotten off to a good start.

When she arrived at the restaurant she found Juliana seated at a banquette where everyone could see her.

They kissed each other on both cheeks.

"Is Marek away?" Juliana asked.

"How can you tell?"

"By looking at your face."

She sat down, trying to erase the look of worry that Juliana had seen. "Yeah, he's in Poland working on the foreign debt problem."

"They should default and get it over with."

"Russia doesn't want them to default."

"America doesn't want Brazil to default," Juliana said, "but sooner or later Brazil will default."

"Well, I don't understand it," Eva said. "At times I wonder if it's only a game."

"It *is* a game. It's one of those games boys play. But let's not talk about them. Tell me how your course is going."

"It's going fine. We're studying Jung now."

"I like Jung. I think he had more useful insights than Freud."

"I like the way he includes religion in his theory. I feel he could be talking about my patron saint when he says that prizes are always given for achievement and not for achieving a higher level of consciousness."

"What about you? Does he talk about you?"

"I think he does. I mean, when he talks about avoiding the past or the future. He says you have to embrace them both in order to achieve a higher level of consciousness."

"You have to reconcile them."

"I haven't done that," Eva admitted.

At that moment the waiter brought a bottle of wine, opened it, and poured it. When he had left them Juliana asked: "What in your past haven't you embraced?"

"My father," Eva said without hesitation.

"What about him?"

She had nothing to fear by telling Juliana, who would never meet her parents. "I just can't forgive my father for what he did to my mother."

"What did he do to her?"

"He cheated on her."

"I should have guessed."

"Why should you have guessed?"

"A lot of husbands cheat on their wives."

"They do? Did your father cheat on your mother?"

Juliana nodded. "Cheating on your wife is acceptable behavior in Brazil. In fact, it's expected."

"Your mother *expected* your father to cheat on her?"

"She must have because she wasn't surprised."

"You mean she found out about it?"

"He wasn't good at hiding it."

"Well, I don't think my mother knows."

"If she doesn't know, then how did it hurt her?"

"By betraying her trust."

"Then she must have expected him to be faithful to her."

"She expected him to keep his vows."

"Well, my mother didn't expect my father to be faithful to her, so in that sense it didn't hurt her."

"Still, it must have hurt her."

"It did. But she survived."

After pausing to take a sip of wine Eva asked: "Do you expect your husband to be faithful to you?"

"Oh, yes," Juliana said. "He's not a Brazilian, thank God."

"Well, I expect my husband to be faithful to me." But as soon as she had said this, Eva remembered the mysterious phone call from the woman who wouldn't leave a message.

"What is it?" Juliana asked.

"Oh, nothing." But wanting to get her friend's opinion, she told Juliana about the phone call.

"Did you ask your husband about it?"

"Yes. He said he didn't know who she was. He said it was probably a student from Poland."

"Why would a student from Poland call him?"

"They know about him. The exiles have a tight community."

"If that's all it is," Julian said, looking at her, "then why are you telling me about it?"

"It made me wonder."

"About what?"

"A lot of things. For one thing, I don't think it was a student from Poland."

"Who do you think it was?"

She had to be careful. "There are people in Poland who don't like what my husband is doing there."

"They don't like bankers interfering with their country?"

"Right. And they could have sent that woman here to lure Marek into a situation where they could harm him."

"This sounds like a spy novel."

"I know. But it's the kind of world we live in."

"I guess it is. You said the phone call made you wonder about a lot of things. What else did it make you wonder about?"

"It made me wonder about my husband. I mean, for a moment I wondered if he knew that woman. But then I felt bad for having suspicions."

"Don't feel bad. From the way that woman acted, any wife would have had suspicions."

"I wish I knew why she called him."

"Well, maybe she *is* a student from Poland. Maybe you're just imagining things to worry about."

"Why would I do that?"

"Because you don't have enough to do."

Eva considered. "Maybe you're right. My mother had a saying about idle minds."

"My mother did too. *Uma mente ociosa é a oficina do diabo.*"

"What does that mean?"

"An idle mind is the devil's workshop."

"Really? That's what my mother's saying means. *Bezczynności umysł jest diabła warsztatu.*"

"So stop worrying about that phone call."

"I will," Eva said—unless the woman called again.

The woman didn't call again, but the two men were standing on the street, watching the house, the next time Lukasz and Czeslaw came for dinner. When Eva saw them she called Marek to the window so that he could see them for himself.

He made a phone call, and about ten minutes later she heard the screech of car wheels, followed by the cries of people being hurt. He wouldn't let her stand at the window to see what was happening, but the next morning she found blood stains on the sidewalk, along with a fragment of tooth.

"What happened to those men?" she asked him that evening. They were sitting at the dining room table eating leftovers from the night before. It was the first time there had ever been leftovers from dinner with Lukasz and Czeslaw. What had happened on the street must have taken away their appetites, and they even refused to take doggy bags.

"We roughed them up," Marek said. "But we didn't hurt them badly. We hurt them just enough to give them a message."

"What if they retaliate?"

"They won't. They know we could have killed them."

"I hope you're not involved in killing people."

"I'm not. But sooner or later I might not have a choice."

"If you kill people," Eva said, "then how are you any different from them?"

"We're doing it for Poland."

"They think they're doing it for Poland."

"They're *not* doing it for Poland. They're doing it for money and power."

"And you're doing it for ideas. Does that make you better?"

"The communists killed for ideas. But they had the wrong ideas. We have the right ideas."

"And what are the right ideas?"

"By now you should know."

"Well, tell me again."

"Liberty and justice," Marek said with passion. "It's the same thing your country fought for in its war against the British. And that's what attracted Kościuszko and Pulaski. They were fighting for the same thing in their war against the Russians."

"So you're picking up where they left off."

"That's right. And we're going to achieve their dream. If we have to kill some people to get there, it's worth the price."

She didn't argue, though she wondered if any ideas were worth the price of a single human life.

A few days later he went back to Poland, and when he returned he had another meeting with Lukasz and Czeslaw. He reported that they had found a way to ship arms into Poland and get them into the hands of the men they had recruited for the underground army. They had about two thousand volunteers, mostly students who had been attracted by the mission of protecting their leaders from the government. Unlike the armies that had evolved from student activist groups in Latin America, they wouldn't attack the government or the military. They would only protect their leaders from the secret police.

"The way things are going," Marek said as they sat in the living room, drinking brandy, "we should have an army of two thousand men by the end of June."

"Unless Jaruzelski finds out what we're doing," Lukasz said.

"When you involve so many people," Czeslaw said, "you always have the risk of having an informer."

"We screened the people carefully," Marek said. "But you can never be a hundred percent sure about people. So we do have the risk that Jaruzelski will find out what we're doing."

"And if he does, he might accelerate his plan."

"His plan isn't ready yet, and he's still waiting for a positive response from Russia."

"What if we do have an informer?" Lukasz asked.

"The damage would be limited," Marek said. "There are only a few people who know the whole plan. The people involved in recruiting the army don't know where the arms are coming from, and the people involved in importing the arms don't know where they're going. So if we have an informer, he could only affect one link in the chain."

"We could have more than one informer," Czeslaw said.

"We could. But if we catch one, we'll make an example of him for the others."

Eva didn't ask how they would do that. She didn't want to know. But she prayed that they wouldn't have an informer.

When she went to the window and looked out she didn't see the two men standing on the sidewalk, watching the house. She concluded that they had gotten the message. And she let down her guard a little.

The next evening after class she shared a taxi with Francis, who let her off on Baker Street. There were no leftovers from the night before since the boys had recovered their appetites, but she had the ingredients to make a pasta, so she didn't have to stop and buy food.

She was crossing Blandford Street when she happened to see Marek walking away from her, heading toward Gloucester Place. He was with a woman, a blond woman.

Feeling as she had when she saw her father go into the hotel with a woman, she stopped dead in the middle of the street—and was almost hit by a taxi. The driver honked his horn, which broke the spell, and with her heart pounding she got out of the street and stood on the sidewalk.

By then Marek and the woman were halfway to Gloucester Place, and Eva couldn't tell anything more about the woman than that she was blond. Was she young? Was she pretty? Was she the woman who had called her husband?

Since she knew that he expected her to come home around this time, she assumed that he wouldn't go anywhere with the woman. He would put her into a taxi and then walk back. She didn't want to wait for him to return, so she resumed walking to Manchester Street, intending to ask him about the woman when he got home.

She told herself that what she had seen wasn't like seeing her father go into a hotel with a woman, but she still couldn't help feeling like she had then.

FIVE

IT DIDN'T TAKE Eva long to get settled into her job at New York Hospital. She was treated well by her supervisors, and she was stimulated by the variety of patients under her care. She worked hard, she learned a lot, and she loved what she was doing. She was carrying out her life's mission.

She quickly realized how important it was to speak and understand Spanish, and since her changing schedule made it almost impossible to enroll in a course, she bought a book on conversational Spanish that came with tapes, and she began teaching herself the language. She got a lot of help from Ramona, who patiently corrected her pronunciation, engaged her in practice conversations, and taught her words that weren't in the book.

"Where does it hurt?" Ramona drilled her at the kitchen table.

"Dónde te duele?" Eva said, trying to pronounce the words as Ramona did.

"Does it hurt when you move it?"

"Te duele cuando lo mueves?"

"Is the pain worse?"

"Es el dolor peor?

"You're beginning to sound like a Puerto Rican."

"Then the patients will understand me."

"Not if they're from Spain. The Spanish speak differently. But we don't get many Spanish patients, so don't worry. Do you have to go to the bathroom?"

"Tienes que ir al cuarto de baño?"

"That's what the book says, but we say *hacer pipi.*"

"Tienes que hacer pipi?"

"Do you have to take a shit?"

"You wouldn't ask a patient that in English."

"All right. Do you have to perform a bowel movement?"

"Tienes que hacer una evacuación?"

"A kid wouldn't understand that. We say *hacer caca.*"

"Tienes que hacer caca?"

"Good. If you want to call someone a shit, the word is *mierda.*"

"Es una mierda."

"Very good. There are worse things you can call people," Ramona said, "and I'll teach them to you—as long as you promise not to use them."

"If I'm not going to use them," Eva asked, "why learn them?"

"So you can understand what people are saying."

Ramona also introduced her to Puerto Rican food. The first Saturday after Eva moved into the apartment, Ramona took her shopping in the Barrio, where she bought things she couldn't get from the supermarket, including pink beans, yucca, plantains, and mangos from a produce store and coffee, cheese, guava paste, and annatto seeds from another store.

They ate *cuchifritos* with rice and beans at a small restaurant, where everyone seemed to know Ramona.

"I love this place," Ramona said. "It's my favorite restaurant in New York."

"I can see that you love this neighborhood," Eva said. "Why did you leave it?"

"I wanted to live closer to the hospital. But I also wanted to get away from where I grew up. If I'd stayed here, I'd always be Don Pedro's daughter."

"I understand. If I'd stayed where I grew up, I'd always be Pan Władysław's daughter."

"So we both wanted to get away from where we grew up. But you were more adventurous. You moved a thousand miles away. I only moved forty blocks away."

"I had a reason."

Ramona waited, munching on a piece of fried pork.

Eva hesitated and then decided to tell her friend. "I had to get away from my father. I caught him cheating on my mother."

"You caught him with a woman?"

"I saw him go into a hotel with a woman."

"That must have hurt."

"It did," Eva said. "But not as much as it would have hurt my mother if she'd found out. So I couldn't tell her. I had to pretend I didn't know."

"And you couldn't face her, knowing what you knew."

"No. I couldn't. I had to get away."

Ramona reflected, poking her fork at what was left of the rice and beans on her plate. "I don't know if my father has cheated on my mother, and I don't want to know. But if he's like other Puerto Rican men, he probably has. Puerto Rican men all cheat on their wives."

"They do?" Eva was shocked.

"Well, that's what they say."

"You mean they talk about it?"

"They always talk about women. Baseball and women, their national sports."

"Would you ever marry a Puerto Rican man?"

"Not in a million years. I know what they're like."

"I wouldn't marry a Polish man."

"Then who are we going to marry?"

"I don't know. I'm not in any hurry to get married. In fact, I can't imagine being married."

"I can't either," Ramona said. "I like being single. I like being in charge of my life."

It turned out that although Ramona had moved only forty blocks away from home, her parents had moved fifteen miles away. They now lived in Yonkers, where they had bought a house. After working for years in a body shop for someone else her father had saved enough to buy his own business, which was located in Yonkers. It was on Saw Mill River Road among a concentration of shops that repaired cars.

Ramona went to see her family about once a month when she had a Saturday or a Sunday off. She invited Eva to come with her one Sunday late in June when they were both off. They went to a morning mass at St. Jean Baptiste, and then they took the subway down to Grand Central, where they caught a train for Yonkers.

Ramona's father met them at the station. Eva could see at a glance that Ramona took after her father, who had the same color hair, eyes, and skin as well as the same manner that let people know he was tough.

"I'm pleased to meet you," he told Eva with a heavy accent.

"*Mucho gusto,*" she said, using her Spanish.

"*Hablas español?*" he asked.

"Only a little. Ramona's teaching me."

"Well, watch out. She'll teach you words that could get you into trouble." He said this as if he were proud of his daughter for not being prissy.

As they approached his car, which he had left in front of the station, Eva noticed an American flag decal on the rear bumper. It was a Ford, which didn't surprise her since Ramona had said that her father would never buy anything but an American car. In that respect he was like her father.

The house was only about five minutes from the station. It was on Alder Street, one of several streets in the neighborhood that were named for trees. In size and style the houses reminded Eva of the neighborhood where she had grown up.

"I hear you're Polish," Ramona's father said as they got out of the car. "We have Polish neighbors. They're good people."

"Twenty years ago this was a Polish neighborhood," Ramona said. "Polish and Italian."

"Now it's Puerto Rican," her father said.

"There are also Dominicans."

"But they're not Americans like us."

Ramona didn't comment, but as her father headed toward the house she rolled her eyes at Eva as if to say: "You see what I had to deal with?"

They found Ramona's mother in the kitchen preparing food. Her mother spoke less English than her father, presumably because she worked at home raising children. There were three children: Ramona and her two younger brothers. Eva thought that Ramona was lucky because she had only two brothers instead of three.

Outside the back door was a patio, where a table was set up for lunch. Ramona stayed in the kitchen to help her mother, while Eva was told to go out and sit down.

She went out to the patio, where Ramona's father introduced her to two boys who were already sitting at the table, ready to eat. Pedro, whom they called Junior, looked about seventeen, and Miguel looked about thirteen.

"You want a soda?" the father asked.

"Yes, please." She had learned that in New York they called soft drinks soda, not pop.

"Are you a nurse like my sister?" Miguel asked.

"Yes. We work on the same floor of the hospital."

"I want to be a doctor."

"That's good."

"I want to be a mechanic," Junior said.

"Mechanics make more money than body shop workers," the father said, placing a bottle of soda on the table in front of Eva.

"But doctors make more than mechanics," Miguel said.

"What do nurses make?" Junior asked.

"Enough to live on," Eva said. "But I don't do it for money. I do it for love."

"You gotta love what you're doing," the father agreed.

A few minutes later Ramona started bringing out the food. The first platter she set on the table had packets wrapped in coarse wet leaves.

"These are *pasteles,*" Ramona said. "They have mashed plantain and meat inside them. They're a lot of work, so we only have them on special occasions."

Realizing that her coming for dinner was the special occasion, Eva reached for a *pastel.*

"The wrapper is a banana leaf. You don't eat that."

"I'm glad you told me. I would have eaten it."

Miguel giggled at the thought of her eating a banana leaf.

As they watched her, Eva unwrapped the packet of dough that had evidently been boiled in the banana leaf. She ate a bite and liked it. "Did I taste a raisin?"

Ramona nodded. "My mom likes to put raisins in them. Every family has its own recipe, and she has her secret ingredients."

"They're sort of like stuffed cabbage," Eva said. "Except that with cabbage we eat the leaves."

"Miguel ate a leaf when he was little. He almost choked on it."

Miguel looked as if he still relished the attention he had gotten.

"Ramona saved him," Junior said.

"I performed a Heimlich maneuver."

"It's a good thing she knew how to do that," the father said.

"How old were you then?" Eva asked, impressed.

"About the same age as Miguel is now. I always wanted to be a nurse, so I learned how to do things as early as possible."

Ramona went back into the kitchen and brought more food. Her mother finally joined them at the table, and they passed the platters, all talking at the same time.

On the way to the train station Ramona's father made a detour to drive by the Polish Center, a turreted building that looked as if it had once been an armory.

"That's where the Polish get together," he said. "They come back to the old neighborhood and have parties there."

It made Eva think of the Polish-American Club, where they still had parties, as her mother told her in their weekly phone calls. After what it had cost her to get out of there, she couldn't imagine going back to the old neighborhood.

Being low on the totem pole, Eva and Ramona had schedules that allowed senior nurses to be off for holidays if they wished, and they were both scheduled to work on the Fourth of July, which came on a Sunday that year. A few days before the holiday a senior nurse who had no plans offered to trade with Ramona, knowing that it was a big event for Ramona's father, so Eva was working the four-to-twelve shift that day without her friend.

Around six in the evening a woman from the Barrio brought a little boy to the emergency room. The child was screaming, the mother was terrified, and no one could understand them.

A nurse from the emergency room called the pediatrics floor, looking for Ramona, who according to the schedule was on duty. Upon learning that Ramona wasn't there, the nurse asked if anyone else on the floor spoke Spanish. At the time Eva was standing by the nursing desk, checking a record, and the nurse who took the call noticed her.

"Do you speak Spanish?" the nurse asked her.

"A little," she said. Like a sponge, she had been absorbing Spanish from Ramona.

"Then go to the emergency room. They need someone who speaks Spanish."

Eva rushed to the emergency room, where the doctor and the nurse were trying in vain to understand what the mother was saying. It didn't help that the mother was hysterical and that the little boy was screaming his head off.

"*Dígame*," Eva said to the mother. "*Qué pasó?*"

The mother was calmed by the sound of her language.

"*No sé.* I think he swallowed something."

"Do you have any idea what it was?"

"It could have been a *palillo*."

Eva didn't know what *palillo* meant, but she tried to figure it out. She knew that *palo* meant stick, and that the suffix *illo* meant small. A small stick? What kind of small stick could you swallow? "Was it a matchstick?"

"*No, no. Un palillo de dientes.*"

"A toothpick?" Eva asked, making a gesture of picking at her teeth. "Was it a toothpick?"

"Yes, I think so. They were using toothpicks for the *albóndigas*, and he must have eaten the toothpick with a meatball."

"What did she say?" the doctor asked. Like Eva, he was low on the totem pole or he wouldn't have been working on the Fourth of July.

"She thinks he swallowed a toothpick," Eva told him.

"That would explain a lot of things," the nurse said.

"It would certainly explain why the kid's in pain," the doctor said. "It might have pierced his intestine. And if it hasn't, it probably will. So we have to get it out."

Eva watched while they prepared to take the little boy to an operating room.

"Thank you so much," the nurse said to Eva. "You may have saved his life."

The next time she saw the little boy he was being wheeled down the hall on his way from the recovery room to a room on her floor.

She followed the gurney into the room, which he would share with a boy who was recovering from a complicated surgery on his leg to repair an injury he had suffered from a car accident. That little boy was five and a half.

For the next few days she took care of the little boy who had swallowed a toothpick. Now that he wasn't screaming his head off, he was very sweet. He had big dark innocent eyes that tugged at her heart. And every time his mother came to visit him, which was often—she would have spent the night in his room if the hospital had allowed it—she thanked Eva and invoked God's blessings upon her.

Hearing about what she had done, but not from her, Ramona caught her leaving the little boy's room and said: *"Felicitaciones!* You passed your first test in Spanish."

They were sitting at the dinner table when Eva said: "I saw you with a woman on Blandford Street. You were walking with her toward Gloucester Place."

"Oh, that was Nadzia," Marek said as if it were a matter of no consequence. "She's a student from Poland, a political refugee who needs help."

"So you were helping her."

"What did you think I was doing?"

"I don't know."

"Did you think I was having an affair with her?"

"No. I just wondered."

"Well, I'm not having an affair with her, but what if I was?"

She didn't follow. "What do you mean?"

"If I was having an affair with her," he said, looking at her closely, "would you still love me?"

"Is this some kind of test?"

"You promised to love me no matter what I did."

"I *would* love you no matter what you did," she affirmed. "But you don't have to test me."

"Why don't I have to test you?"

"Because you can trust me."

"I know I can. In fact, you're the only person I can trust. But I can't trust myself. And I'm afraid I might do something that would make you stop loving me."

"You don't have to worry. I wouldn't stop loving you."

"No matter what I did?"

"No matter what you did. But I hope you don't kill anyone," she added, naming the worst thing he could do.

"Well, I might have to kill someone."

"Why would you have to?"

"To stop him from killing me."

His reply aroused the fear that she had shared with Juliana. "Remember when that woman called you and didn't leave a message? Was that Nadzia?"

"Yes. It was. But why are you bringing her up again?"

"Because I have a feeling that the secret police sent her to stop you from accomplishing your mission."

"The secret police?" He laughed at the thought. "They didn't send her. She escaped from them."

"I still don't trust her."

"You don't trust her because she's a woman."

"Maybe that's why. But I don't trust her. And if I were you, I wouldn't tell her anything."

"I only tell her what she has to know."

"I wouldn't tell her anything."

"All right. I'll be careful with her."

"And I'll pray that they didn't send her."

"Do you really believe that God answers your prayers?"

"Sometimes He does. And so far He's always answered my prayer that you'll get home safely."

"What if I didn't get home safely?" Marek asked. "Would you still believe in God?"

"Yes," she said definitely.

"So you believe in God no matter what He does?"

"My faith in God is unconditional."

"And your love for me is unconditional?"

"Yes. Well, I should qualify that. My faith in God and my love for you are as unconditional as they can be in someone who's only human."

"Then they have limits?"

"Of course they do."

"Has your faith ever been pushed to the limit?"

She thought about it. Seeing her father go into the hotel with that woman had pushed her faith, but not to the limit. Seeing children mangled and dying had pushed it further. But beyond the normal moments of doubt, she couldn't think of anything that had pushed her faith to the limit. "No. It hasn't been."

"Then it hasn't been tested."

"Why does it have to be tested?"

"To prove it," he told her.

"I don't have to prove my faith. God knows I believe in Him."

"What about your love?"

"I don't have to prove it. You know I love you."

He shook his head. "I don't know anything."

Later, in bed she gave him what she hoped was convincing evidence of her love for him.

After their last class, instead of dropping her off on Baker Street, Francis suggested that they have dinner together to celebrate completing the course. She had mentioned that her husband was away, so Francis knew she didn't have to go directly home.

If Francis hadn't been a priest she would have hesitated to have dinner with him, wondering what he might have in mind. But she knew there would be no problem with him, so she accepted the suggestion.

He had the driver drop them off on Wigmore Street, which was in her neighborhood, and he led her to a pub that she had passed many times.

"This is an Irish pub," he told her, opening the door for her.

"How do you know?" she asked, entering the place. It smelled of beer and damp wood.

"I've been here many times."

"You were in my neighborhood and you didn't let me know?"

"You wouldn't have wanted to be with us."

Since Francis was Irish, she wondered if he was involved with the IRA, which had claimed responsibility for a series of bombings in London during the 1970s. There hadn't been a bombing in London since 1979, but the problem in Northern Ireland hadn't been resolved, so there was always the possibility that the bombings would resume.

She realized that although she had sat next to Francis in class for ten weeks and had shared taxis with him, she didn't know much about him.

Francis led her to a booth in the back of the pub, where they sat down opposite each other.

"What would you like to drink?" he asked.

"I'll have a beer," she said, assuming that people didn't drink wine in this place.

"A lager or a bitter?"

"A lager. I don't like bitter."

He smiled understandingly. "Most Americans don't like bitter. They like their beer cold and fizzy."

A young man came to their booth and asked: "What'll you be having tonight, father?"

"A lager and a Guinness," Francis told him.

When the waiter had left them, Eva asked: "Why wouldn't I have wanted to be with you?"

"Because you must hear more than enough talk about politics."

She had told him that her husband was Polish, and that he worked for a bank and made a lot of trips to Poland, but nothing more. "Why do you think that?"

"I know some Polish exiles, and all they talk about is politics."

"My husband isn't a Polish exile. He's an American."

"I'll bet he thinks of himself as an exile."

"He does," she admitted, knowing he didn't think of himself as an American. "And I do hear more than enough about Polish politics. But I wouldn't mind hearing about Irish politics."

"It's all the same. Whether it's Poland or Ireland or any other part of the world, it's always about resources. I mean, fighting over them instead of sharing them. The problem is, people aren't willing to share resources."

"Why aren't they?" she asked, remembering how her brothers used to fight over toys, territory, and parental attention.

"They believe there aren't enough resources for everyone. But there are," Francis said, making a gesture with open hands, "as long as people share them. If they fight over them, they waste resources, and then there really aren't enough. And the more they fight, the more reason they have to fight."

The waiter brought their drinks and they both ordered fish and chips, which Francis recommended.

"Well, I don't know if what you say applies to Poland," Eva said after taking a sip of beer. "You can't expect the Poles to share resources with the Russians."

"In that situation it's about the land that stretches from the German border to Siberia. If the Russians were willing to share that land, they'd let the Poles have their piece of it. But they want it all, including a major piece of Germany."

"Why do the Russians want it all? They have so much land without Poland."

"They feel they need it," Francis said. "They feel they need as much land as possible between them and the West."

"You mean because the West might attack them?"

"It attacked them in the past."

"Were those wars about resources?"

"Yes. They were. Napoleon and Hitler wanted to control as much land as possible."

She took another sip of beer. "And what about Ireland?"

"The problem there," Francis said, "is a legacy of the English wanting to control as much land as possible and building a vast empire. Northern Ireland is one of the few remaining pieces of that empire. And the Irish want independence from the English just as the Polish want independence from the Russians."

"So it's a similar situation."

"It's similar, but the Irish situation is a bit more complicated. You see, there are two groups in Northern Ireland fighting over resources—the Catholics and the Protestants. In the eyes of the Catholics, the Protestants are colonizers who don't belong in Ireland, and in the eyes of the Protestants, the Catholics are rabble who want the rewards they didn't work for. Imagine what would have happened in your country if instead of fighting the English for independence, your people had fought each other over resources."

"We would have had a class war."

"And if the underclass had won, you would have had a revolution. Instead, you had only a war of independence."

"So both types of war are going on in Northern Ireland?"

Francis nodded. "That's what makes the situation complicated."

"Are you from Northern Ireland?"

"No. I'm from Dublin."

"Then you're not involved."

"I'm not involved in the politics, but I *am* involved."

"When you said I wouldn't have wanted to be with you," she said, smiling, "I imagined you plotting with the IRA to blow up the Tower of London."

"You did? Well, that's not far from the truth. The truth is, I meet with people from the Irish community, who may or may not be connected with the IRA, and I try to make them realize that blowing up the Tower of London isn't the solution."

"Is that your assignment from the church?"

"My assignment from the church is to assist at a parish in East London and to serve people in the usual ways. But that leaves room for what you call outreach."

"You reach out to people from the Irish community who don't attend church?"

"I meet them wherever I can find them."

"What's your mission?"

"My mission," Francis said compellingly, "is to get people to realize that they can't solve the problem with violence."

"So how can they solve it?"

"By sharing resources. The Protestants have to share what they have, and the Catholics have to settle for less than everything. They have to meet each other halfway."

"Well, I can see how that would apply to Poland. There are people who've collaborated with the Russians, and they don't want to share what they've gained."

"I didn't consider that aspect," Francis admitted. "They're like the Protestants who collaborated with the English. So maybe the two situations aren't that different."

"Maybe they aren't."

"Except that the Polish haven't yet resorted to violence."

"No. They haven't. But they might."

Francis gave her a look as if he thought she might know more than she was telling him, but he didn't press it. He only said: "Let's pray that they don't."

"Let's," she said, joining him in a silent prayer.

When Marek returned from Poland she could tell that something had gone wrong. He went into the kitchen, poured a shot of vodka, gulped it down, refilled his glass, and then went into the living room and sank into the sofa.

Sitting down beside him, Eva asked: "What happened?"

"The police intercepted the shipment of arms."

"So they must have known about it."

"They did. Someone betrayed us."

"Do you know who it was?"

"I have no idea," Marek said glumly. He held his glass against his chin. "It could have been anyone."

"You don't trust anyone?"

"I trust some people."

"Then it couldn't have been anyone."

"I trust Lukasz, and I trust Czeslaw. And I trust a few people in Poland."

"Well, that narrows the list."

"It does. But not much."

"How many people knew about the shipment?"

He counted, murmuring: "*Jeden, dwa, trzy, cztery, pięć—*"

She waited, wanting to help him.

"Nine," he finally said. "Not including the people who sold us the arms and the people who brought them into the country."

"You don't suspect those people?"

"They're business people. They want to make money. So it wouldn't make sense for them to betray us."

"How many of the nine people are in London?"

"Lukasz, Czeslaw, and myself. The others are in Poland."

"Then you've narrowed the list to six people. Do you know all of them well?"

"I know some of them well."

"Then you could narrow the list further."

Marek considered. "I don't have to tell all of them about the next shipment. Only three of them have to know about it. So if the police find out about the next shipment, we only have to kill three people."

"I hope you don't mean that," Eva said, shocked.

"I do mean it. If one of them betrays us, we can't take any more chances. We don't have time."

"But if you killed all three of them, you'd kill two innocent people. And you wouldn't even know if one of them was guilty, so you might kill three innocent people."

"In a war you can't help killing innocent people."

Eva didn't accept this justification, but instead of arguing she looked for a way around the problem. "You wouldn't have to kill any of them if you didn't tell them about the next shipment."

"No. We wouldn't," Marek agreed. "And maybe we don't have to tell them. But sooner or later we'll have to kill someone. So I hope you won't judge me."

"I won't ever judge you, but God will."

"I thought He forgave everything."

"He does. But only if you ask for His forgiveness."

"I wouldn't do that since I don't believe in Him. But I *would* ask for your forgiveness."

"You wouldn't have to. I told you, I won't ever judge you."

Marek looked as if he wanted to believe her.

SIX

ONE OR TWO evenings a week, if they were both off, Ramona and Eva went to the Recovery Room or other bars in the neighborhood like the Red Blazer, the Mad Hatter, or Drake's Drum. These bars were places where girls could go, usually in pairs but sometimes in groups of three or four, without feeling that they had stepped over a line and intruded into the male domain of a typical bar. They were places where girls could safely hang out and, if they wanted, meet guys.

Ramona and Eva were open to the idea of meeting guys, but they were very particular. They were willing to talk with guys while sitting at the bar or standing in the crowd in front of the bar, but whenever a pair of guys asked them to go somewhere and have dinner with them or go to someone's apartment, they went to the women's room and held a conference, at which they decided that neither of them was interested in either of the guys, and they returned and declined the invitation. They had an agreement that if one of them was interested in a guy, the other would go along with her as far as having company would be useful and then make an excuse for leaving. They also had an agreement that if a guy began to annoy one of them, the other would help her get rid of him.

After nursing two drinks and spending a few hours in a bar, they would pay up and go to a local restaurant for dinner. There were a lot of restaurants to choose from, but they preferred a Chinese restaurant on Second Avenue, where along with the moo shoo pork or chicken with fish flavor or shrimp with black bean sauce they drank pots of tea. And while they ate they discussed the guys who had tried to pick them up.

"He was kind of cute," Ramona said about a guy who had approached her at the Red Blazer one evening, "but he was so stupid. Imagine asking me where I got my tan."

"Mine was just as stupid," Eva said about the guy who had approached her. "He asked me if pediatrics had something to do with bicycles."

"It makes you wonder if they went beyond third grade."

"Mine claimed he had an MBA from Columbia."

"Mine said he went to Yale. I was supposed to be impressed."

"If they're typical of the guys who graduate from those places, then we're in trouble."

"You mean you and me?"

"I mean our country. They don't want to do anything except make money."

"And have sex with girls they meet in bars."

"That's the problem. They have only one thing in mind."

"Well, I can't imagine having sex with that guy," Ramona said with a shudder.

"I can't either," Eva said, referring to the other guy.

Of course neither of them had ever had sex with anyone. Neither of them had any intention of having sex until she was married. And neither of them had even been in a situation where the idea had entered her mind.

By the end of that summer they both decided that instead of wasting their time in bars, they would enroll in Hunter College and pursue bachelor's degrees in nursing. The classes were in the evenings, and with their changing schedules they couldn't always make the classes, but usually one of them could cover for the other, so they were able to do together what they couldn't have done separately. Between their jobs and going to college, they were fully occupied, and they had little time to worry about guys. In their minds there was no guy who couldn't wait.

They were both scheduled to work on Christmas, so for Eva there was no point in going home. On Christmas Eve, instead of celebrating *Wigilia* with her family, she had dinner with Ramona at the Green Kitchen at one in the morning after going off duty.

On Christmas Day before going on duty she went to mass with Ramona at St. Jean Baptiste, and then she called her mother and wished her *Wesołych Świąt*.

More than two years passed, and during that time Eva was happier than she had ever been. She loved her work, and she was doing well at Hunter College. In May she would graduate with a bachelor's in nursing, which would increase her salary and move her up the totem pole, though she didn't care about moving up. She was happy where she was, caring for patients and doing little things for them, following the path to holiness that St. Thérèse had showed her, committed to her mission.

Then something happened that changed everything.

She and Ramona were in the Recovery Room, celebrating the fact that they had completed the program at Hunter, when a guy appeared in front of Eva out of nowhere. She was sitting on a barstool, and he approached her like a homeless person looking for a handout, appealing to her with a bottomless need in his dark eyes. For a long, long time he gazed at her as if she was the answer to his prayers.

Finally, in an accent that she associated with displaced persons, he told her: "Only you can save me."

"Save you from what?"

"From the darkness of unending night."

If it hadn't been for that look in his eyes she might have laughed. Among the guys who had tried to pick her up, there had been a few who professed to be poets. But they had never gone so far. "Well, I don't think you have the right person."

"I know I do," he said with conviction.

"How would you know? You just met me."

"I feel like I've known you all my life."

"But you haven't," she said, trying to resist. "And you don't know a thing about me."

"I know you're a nurse."

"All the girls in this bar are nurses."

"I know you're sympathetic."

"I'm sympathetic with children in the hospital, but not with guys I meet in bars."

"Then let's have dinner, so you can get to know me."

"Why would I want to get to know you?"

"Because you never met anyone like me before."

Feeling exposed, she shied away from his unremitting gaze and turned to her friend.

"*Tengo que hacer pipi,*" Ramona said. "You want to join me?"

"Yes, I do," she replied in Spanish.

She climbed off the stool and walked around the guy and headed for the women's room with Ramona.

With the door locked behind them, Ramona asked: "Do you want to get rid of him?"

"I don't know. You think I should?"

"There's something I don't like about him."

"Did you hear what he said?"

"Yeah, what a line."

"You think it's a line?"

"Only you can save me," Ramona said, imitating his accent. "And you know how? By having sex with him. That's all he wants."

"I think he wants more than that."

"Yeah. He wants to have sex with you more than once, but then he'll drop you like a hot *pastel.*"

"Is that what you think?"

"That's what I feel."

She had a feeling that Ramona was right, but she wanted to find out for herself. "He asked me to have dinner with him so I can get to know him."

"Yeah, I heard. And after dinner he'll ask you to go to his apartment."

"But I don't have to go with him."

"If a guy like that can talk you into having dinner with him," Ramona said with obvious concern, "he can talk you into going to his apartment."

"Oh, he can't talk me into doing that."

"I think he can. I saw how he got to you."

"He didn't get to me."

"Then why would you have dinner with him?"

"I don't know. I guess I want to know if he really meant it."

"When he said you could save him?"

"Yeah. Does that sound crazy?"

"It does to me. I hope you still don't want to be a saint."

"I don't," she insisted. "I gave up that idea a long time ago."

"So what if he really did mean it? What would you do? Would you try to save him?"

"Why are you asking so many questions?"

"Because there's something I don't like about that guy, and I don't want you to get hurt."

"Well, I'd only have dinner with him."

"I think you should get rid of him."

Not without misgivings, Eva finally made a decision. "I'm going to have dinner with him."

"All right. But please be careful."

"I will. Don't worry."

As she went out of the women's room she almost hoped that the guy had left, having gotten tired of waiting for her. But he was still there.

Approaching him she realized that he was only about two inches taller than her, which made him about five feet three, short for a man, but he looked as if he would be hard to push around. The sleeves of his loose white shirt were rolled up, revealing powerful hairy forearms.

"So what did you decide?" he asked anxiously.

"I decided to have dinner with you."

His face glowed, and there was a light of hope in his eyes. "You did? Good. There's an excellent restaurant only a few blocks from here."

"What's it called?" Ramona asked.

"Vašata," he said. "It's a Czech restaurant."

"Are you Czech?"

"No. But I like Czech food."

"I'm her roommate," Ramona told him, implying that he would have to deal with her.

"It's nice to meet you," the guy mumbled, obviously without meaning it. He must have sensed that Ramona didn't like him.

The two girls paid for their drinks and kissed before parting. As she walked away with the guy Eva glanced over her shoulder and saw Ramona following them as if she wanted to know where they were going, just in case.

"Are you Puerto Rican?" the guy asked.

"Why do you ask?"

"You were speaking Spanish."

"I learned it from my roommate. We have a lot of patients who speak Spanish."

They didn't speak again until they got to the restaurant.

He evidently knew the head waiter, with whom he spoke what sounded like Czech. It was similar enough to Polish so that she could understand their exchange.

"Could we have a banquette?" the guy asked.

"Yes, sir. Would you like to sit there?" the head waiter asked, pointing to a corner table.

"That would be perfect."

They followed him to the table, and Eva sat down on the banquette. She positioned herself so that instead of being able to sit next to her the guy had to sit across from her.

The head waiter gave them menus and a wine list. Without looking at the wine list, the guy ordered a bottle of Riesling.

"If you're not Czech, are you German?" Eva asked.

"No, I'm not German," the guy said as if she had insulted him. "Why do you want to know what I am when you don't even know my name?"

"So what's your name?"

"Marek," he said with his head held high.

"Well, that sounds Polish," she said, beginning to wonder what she had gotten herself into. "Are you Polish?"

"Yes. And I'm not Polish-American."

"You mean you're from Poland?"

"I was born and raised there."

"Are you visiting here?"

"No. I live here."

"What do you do?"

"I work for a bank." He named the bank, and he explained that it had branches all over the world. Then he added: "I'm in the department that covers Poland."

"Do you travel to Poland?"

"About once a month."

"What's it like?"

"In its economy it's like a third-world country. But in its culture it's way ahead of this country."

"In what respects?"

"People there know how to read. Of course they're not free to read what they want, but at least they know how to read— unlike most people in this country."

"That's not fair."

"It's my experience."

"Well, if you don't like it here, why do you live here?"

"I have no choice. My father and I were lucky to get out of Poland alive."

Influenced by what Ramona had said, Eva was skeptical. "If that's the case, then how are you able to travel there?"

"Being a banker gives me immunity. The Polish government owes so much money to Western banks, they wouldn't dare hurt a banker. And I'm not the one they care about. My father's the one they care about."

"Why do they care about your father?"

"He organized protests against the government."

"When did he do that?"

"In 1968. It was a big year for protests all over the world."

She remembered her father and his colleagues talking about those protests. She had been only ten at the time. "So you came to this country twelve years ago?"

"Yes. I was fourteen. I wasn't old enough to be involved in the protests. But I had to leave because of my father."

"What about your mother?"

He stared at her as if he didn't know what the word meant.

There was a long silence, during which she felt bad. She figured that something had happened to his mother, and she would have told him she was sorry, but she didn't know exactly what she should be sorry for. She only knew she should be sorry for asking about his mother.

"What's your name?" he asked, changing the subject.

"Eva," she said, pronouncing it the American way

"Eva," he said, pronouncing it the Polish way.

"My parents are Polish," Eva admitted. "But I was born here, so I'm not Polish."

"You look Polish. *Mówisz po polsku?*"

"Yes. It was my first language."

From that point on they spoke Polish, and she felt as if she had been dragged back into her old neighborhood.

Their waiter brought a bottle of wine, which he opened and poured for Marek to taste.

"That's fine," Marek said in the waiter's language.

When the waiter had left them after pouring some wine into Eva's glass and more wine into Marek's glass, they looked at the menus. The items on the menu didn't look Slavic. In fact, they looked more German than anything.

Raising her eyes, she managed to look at Marek while his eyes were focused on his menu. With his dark hair, pale complexion, and short stature he could have been her brother, in contrast to her real brothers who were blond, pink, and tall.

He looked up and caught her off guard. The bottomless need in his dark eyes, which had appealed to her when he materialized in front of her at the Recovery Room, was still there. And now it fully took hold of her.

There was another long silence, during which she was overwhelmed by a passion to respond to his appeal. Instantly, it became a vocation.

As if he knew she had succumbed, he ended the silence with the mundane comment: "The schnitzel here is excellent."

"I'll have that," she said, accepting the suggestion.

They both ordered schnitzel with potatoes and sauerkraut.

"Where did you go to college?" she asked, trying to make a normal conversation.

"I got my bachelor's at Georgetown, and I got my master's at Johns Hopkins."

"Do you have any brothers or sisters?"

"No. I'm an only child."

"Where does your father live?"

"Arlington. He works for the State Department."

"Is he an American citizen?"

"Yes. And I am too. We were naturalized three years ago. But I'm Polish," he told her as if he wanted to make sure that there was no question about it.

After dinner he didn't ask her to go to his apartment. He walked her home and left her in front of her building, saying that he would call her.

So at least Ramona had been wrong about one thing.

When they came to dinner Lukasz and Czeslaw brought a huge ring of *kielbasa*, the fine-grained sausage that her mother always bought from a local Polish store whose proprietor called himself the Kielbasy King.

Eva cut the sausage into three pieces that would fit into a pot of water, which she brought to a boil while the boys were having shots of vodka. After letting it heat for a few minutes, she took one piece of sausage out of the pot and cut it at angles into slices that they could eat from a plate using toothpicks. For a moment she was reminded of the Puerto Rican boy who had swallowed a toothpick with a meatball, and she missed her work, she missed Ramona, and she missed New York. Since there were no classes until September, she had nothing to do all day. You could only spend so much time reading and going to museums.

She put the slices of *kielbasa* onto a platter and brought it with a dish of mustard into the living room, where she passed it around. After making several rounds she set the platter and the dish on the coffee table and sat down.

They were still talking about the interception of the arms shipment.

"I don't believe any of those people would betray us," Lukasz said. "I know them all, and I have complete confidence in them."

"It has to be one of them," Marek argued.

"Are you sure we've identified all the people who knew about the shipment?" Czeslaw asked.

"I'm sure," Marek said. But to satisfy his colleagues he went over the list, starting with the people involved in the shipment.

"It could be one of those people."

"For them it's business. It's not about politics."

"Yeah, I know. They'd sell arms to kill their own mothers. But if they'd do that, they'd do anything for money. And maybe the Russians are paying one of them more than he's making from the shipment."

"That's a possibility," Lukasz said.

"I guess it is," Marek allowed.

"We can test that hypothesis," Czeslaw said, "by using another source of arms."

"We don't have time to find another source."

"We don't have time to have another shipment intercepted."

"You're right," Marek concluded. "It would be better to lose a few weeks while we find another source of arms than to lose a month if they intercept the next shipment."

"It shouldn't take long to find another source," Czeslaw said. "Everyone's in the arms business. We could probably even buy arms from the Russians. We could pretend they're for guerrillas in Latin America."

"I have some good contacts," Marek said. "I'll sound them out tomorrow. But at the same time I want to limit the number of people in Poland who know about the shipment."

"We can do that," Lukasz said. "But I have no doubts about any of them."

"I have a question," Czeslaw said. "Does the CIA support what we're doing?"

"Of course they support it," Marek said. "They have the same goal that we do."

"Are you sure?"

"I'm sure."

"Well, I was just thinking— If the CIA didn't support it, then they would have a reason to betray us."

"If they didn't support it," Marek said, "the person I report to would tell me."

"Maybe he doesn't know what they want," Czeslaw said.

"You mean the people above him?"

"Yes. They could be playing a different game."

"They're not, believe me," Marek said. "I know their game. It's to overthrow communist governments. I mean, look at what they did in Chile, and look at what they're doing in other Latin American countries."

"But they like military governments," Czeslaw argued, "and Jaruzelski is trying to establish a military government."

"He's trying to establish a *communist* military government."

"It would still be a military government, and if the CIA believes that the alternative is chaos, they might prefer any kind of military government."

Marek shook his head. "The alternative in Poland isn't chaos. The alternative is a stable democracy."

"The CIA might not see that."

"They do, believe me. I know what they see."

"All right," Czeslaw said. "You know them better than I do."

It took Marek only a week to find another source of arms, and the next shipment was scheduled for the middle of August. He went to Poland to make sure that everything was in place, and he planned to return the week before the shipment.

While he was away Eva decided to sign up for another psychology course at Birkbeck, which began in September. She hoped that Francis would be in the course, but she wouldn't know until the classes started. She didn't know how to contact him, and every time she passed the pub where they had had dinner she wondered if he was in there meeting with exiles from Northern Ireland, trying to make them understand that they couldn't solve the problem with violence.

She never went into the pub, but she went often into St. James and prayed in the Lady Chapel with her eyes fixed on the painting of the Blessed Mother. She prayed for other people, beginning with her mother and ending with her father. When she prayed for Marek, she asked God to give him faith. It would not only help Marek, it would also lighten her own burden. It was hard knowing that she was all that stood between him and the darkness of unending night. And when she finally prayed for herself the only thing she ever asked for was the strength to provide the bulwark that her husband needed.

Once a week she called her mother, as she had in New York. It cost a lot more from London, so she tried to limit the calls to twenty minutes. She sometimes went beyond that limit, but Marek never complained about it.

She called on Sundays, which her mother now with years of seniority always had off. She timed her calls so that she would catch her mother at the kitchen table having coffee after doing the dishes from the Sunday dinner that always followed mass at St. Casimir. If her brothers were there, they would be in the living room with their father, watching a game.

Most of what they said in these calls was a repetition of what they had said in previous calls, but it served the purpose of keeping them in touch. There was rarely anything new. Her brothers were still going to school, with two of them in college now, and her father was still working at the Whirlpool plant. There were rumors that Whirlpool was going to close the plant, but they were nothing new. The church was raising money for repairs, but that was nothing new. So when Eva called her mother on the first Sunday of August, she expected the usual conversation. But this time there was something new.

"Your father has a problem," her mother said before they had gone very far.

"What kind of problem?" Eva asked, suddenly upset.

"His doctors are waiting for the results of some tests, but they think it might be lung cancer."

"Oh, my God. When will they know?"

"Within a few days."

"Poor Papa," she said, overcome with sympathy.

"It's from smoking, or from working at that plant," her mother said, trying to explain it.

"A lot of people smoke and work at plants."

"I know. And a lot of people get lung cancer. Would you like to talk with him?"

"Yes," she said, bracing herself. As she waited for him to come to the phone she tried to calm her feelings so that she wouldn't burst out into tears.

"*Witaj,*" her father said in a low voice.

"*Witaj, papa.* How are you?"

"I'm fine. I don't believe what these doctors are saying, so don't worry. How are you?"

"I'm fine," she said, lying as much as she thought he was.

"How's Marek?"

"He's fine. He's in Poland now."

"What's he doing there?"

"The usual things." Her father didn't know what Marek really did. If he had, he might have let it slip out while bragging to his colleagues about his Polish son-in-law.

"Well, give him my best when he returns."

"I will," she said, sensing that her father was about to wind up the conversation. "*Kocham cię, papa.* I love you."

"I love you too. Be a good girl."

She resumed talking with her mother, who ended by promising to let her know what they learned from the tests.

When she prayed for people in the Lady Chapel the next morning she began with her father. Kneeling there, she realized that she still loved her father, even after what he had done to her mother. And she asked God to forgive her for judging him so harshly.

Marek returned from Poland in unusually high spirits. He was confident that they had tightened security to a point where the government wouldn't learn about the next shipment.

She was reluctant to spoil his mood by telling him about her father, but they had agreed to share everything, good or bad, so after he was settled on the sofa with the bottle of vodka and a shot glass, she broke the news to him.

"I'm sorry," he said, taking her hand. "Let's hope the doctors are wrong."

"My father thinks they are, but my mother doesn't. I can tell."

"In any case, you should go home."

"I was thinking I should. Could you go with me?"

He shook his head. "I couldn't now. Things are just now coming to a head."

"Well, I don't want to leave you alone here."

"I'll be all right," he assured her. "But let's wait for the test results. There's always a chance that the doctors are wrong."

She prayed that they were, but at the same time she tried to prepare herself for the worst.

The next day she went to the Lady Chapel and prayed. She spent an hour or more in the church, but then she had all the remaining hours in the day. Before, it had been hard enough not being occupied, but now with her father to worry about and with nothing to distract her, she didn't know what to do with herself.

After walking the streets of Marylebone she wandered over to Regents Park, where she sat on a bench and watched people for a while. Then she walked back to the Wallace, where she spent a few hours before heading home.

It was late afternoon, and the days were getting shorter, but there would still be about four more hours of light. In the summer it stayed light here so much longer than in New York, but then in winter it got dark so much earlier. She hoped that by the winter the problem in Poland would be resolved, so that they could go back to New York. But she had a feeling it would never be resolved.

When she entered the apartment she was tired from walking and from climbing the stairs, and since Marek wouldn't be home for at least two hours, she went into the bedroom and lay down, intending to rest but not to fall asleep.

With her head on the pillow she became aware of an alien smell. It came from the pillow, and sniffing the pillow, she realized that it was perfume. And it wasn't hers.

She sniffed again to make sure it wasn't cologne, a new fragrance that Marek had bought at the duty-free shop while waiting for his plane to take off. But it wasn't men's cologne, it was women's perfume.

SEVEN

WHEN MAREK CALLED her the next day she was on duty, but Ramona answered and took a message asking her to call him back. She found the message in the kitchen on a piece of note paper, the kind from a pad that changed colors about every twenty pieces. The color of this piece happened to be red, one of the colors of the Polish flag.

The message from Ramona said: "That guy called you. He wants you to call him back. Can we talk before you do?"

It was almost one in the morning, so Eva wasn't going to call him now anyway. She was tired, and all she wanted was to go to bed. Ramona had the eight-to-four shift and would get up at seven, which gave her enough time to put herself together and make it to work. So if they were going to talk before she called Marek back, they would have to do it between seven and the time Ramona left, and Eva hadn't planned to wake up that early.

When she opened her eyes several hours later she saw Ramona standing in the doorway of her bedroom brushing her thick dark hair, which she would put up and hold together in a clamp. "Did you get the message?"

"Yeah," Eva said, rubbing her eyes.

"So what happened last night?"

"Well, he didn't ask me to go to his apartment."

"I figured he hadn't. You came home at eleven twenty."

"You checked the time?"

"I couldn't sleep worrying about you."

"But there was nothing to worry about. He took me to dinner at a very nice restaurant, and then he walked me home. He was a perfect gentleman."

"Where did he go to college? Princeton?"

"No. Georgetown."

"I never met a guy from there. But watch out for gentlemen. They look down on us, and they treat us accordingly."

"He didn't act that way," Eva said. "I mean, he was a little intense, but— To tell you the truth, the only thing wrong with him is that he's Polish."

"There must be something else wrong with him."

"I can't see anything. But of course I just met him, and I still don't know much about him."

Ramona began to twist her hair. "Did he talk any more about how you can save him?"

"No. But he made me feel—" It was hard to explain. "When I looked into his eyes, I wanted to save him. And I believed that I *could* save him."

"From the darkness of unending night?"

"I should have asked him to explain that. I wonder if it means that he's an atheist."

"If he is, then you can't help him."

"Why can't I?" she asked, raising her head from the pillow and resting on her elbows.

"You can't give someone faith."

"You can give him love."

"That's not the same." Ramona stopped, holding her hair at the back of her head in a position so that she could clamp it. "You haven't fallen in love with him, have you?"

"I don't know. But something *has* happened to me. I only had dinner with him, but I feel like I made a commitment to him. You know what I mean?"

"I never had that happen to me. I can only imagine."

"I certainly didn't want it to happen," Eva said, fully sitting up now and wrapping her arms around her knees, "especially after I learned that he's Polish."

"I knew he was foreign, but I wouldn't have guessed that he was Polish."

"I wouldn't have either. He doesn't look Polish."

"But he does look kind of like you."

"I know he does. He could be my brother."

"I wouldn't go that far," Ramona said, clamping her hair. "So what are you going to do?"

"I'm going to call him back."

"I shouldn't have given you the message. If you didn't know he called, you wouldn't call him back, and then maybe he would have gone away."

"No, I don't think he would have. I think he would have called again."

"Well, I have to go. I'll see you later."

"Okay. Thanks."

"Thanks for what?"

"For giving me the message."

"I never considered not giving it to you. What do I know? I don't have any more experience with guys than you do. So I could be wrong about him."

Marek had left a home number and a work number. By the time she got up it was almost ten, so she tried the latter. A secretary answered and offered to take a message since Mr. Ostrowski was in a meeting. Eva was repulsed by his last name, and she couldn't imagine herself as Mrs. Ostrowksi.

But she left a message, and she heard from him a half hour later. He wondered if she could have dinner with him that evening. She explained that she was on the four-to-twelve shift for the rest of the week, which ruled out having dinner. She expected him to suggest having lunch, but instead he asked if she could have dinner with him on Sunday, when she was scheduled for the eight-to-four shift. It made her wonder if Ramona had been right since he couldn't have asked her to go to his apartment after lunch. But she accepted.

He took her to a Hungarian restaurant in the East 80's, where in talking with the waiter he demonstrated proficiency in another language, which she didn't understand a word of.

"What other languages do you speak?" she asked when the waiter had left them.

"Besides Polish, Czech, and Hungarian? I speak German, and Russian, and Slovak, and Serbo-Croatian. But it's no big thing. The Slavic languages are similar."

"I guess it's useful in your work."

"It's very useful."

They had goulash, accompanied by a bottle of Bull's Blood wine. While they ate he asked her a lot of questions about her work. He was the first guy who had ever shown an interest in it. Granted, she had never had dinner with a guy before, but the conversations at the bar always revolved around what the guys did. They acted like once they knew she was a nurse, they knew all they needed to know—that she wouldn't have romantic notions about sex. And they proceeded to talk about themselves, trying to impress her.

Marek was different. Though he knew she was a nurse, he didn't act like he only wanted to have sex with her. Of course he wanted something from her, but she had a feeling it was more than what those other guys wanted, and by the end of the meal she believed it was a relationship.

It was only nine when they left the restaurant, too early for him to walk her home, so as they lingered indecisively on the sidewalk, Marek said: "We could go to my apartment. I live only a block from here."

She hesitated, suspecting why he had chosen that restaurant.

"We could talk there," he explained. "It would be more private than going to a bar."

"We would only talk, right?"

"Right. That's all I have in mind," he claimed, gazing at her ingenuously.

"All right," she agreed, trusting him.

They walked to his building, a red brick structure on York Avenue. It had a doorman, who greeted Marek respectfully, and it had an elevator. As they rode up she noticed that the building had twenty floors.

They got out on the fifteenth floor, and Marek led her down the hall to his apartment. She went along with him, remembering how Ramona had warned her.

His apartment had modern furniture that unlike the pieces in her apartment clearly hadn't been collected from the streets. What really struck her was a large banner on the wall, the Polish coat of arms with the white eagle on a red background. It was like the banner that hung in the Polish-American Club back home, and it was almost as large. The eagle, which in Polish was *Orzeł Biały*, looked proud and fierce, though now it didn't scare her as it had when she was a little girl. But it did make an impression on her.

"You like it?" Marek asked her.

"Yeah. I guess." She had mixed feelings about it that she couldn't explain.

"My father brought it with him when we left Poland."

"It must have filled a suitcase."

"It did. There wasn't room for anything else."

She wandered over to the large window that had a view of the East River and the borough of Queens, the lights of which extended as far as she could see. Beyond the lights was the dark ocean. "You have a great view."

"I'm lucky," he said, standing next to her. "Most of the apartments I looked at had views of air shafts and fire escapes."

"How long have you lived here?"

"Only a year. I came to New York after I got my degree from the School of Advanced International Studies."

"Why did you decide to work for a bank?"

"I wanted to travel to Poland and do something there. I could have worked for the State Department, but if I had, I would have been stuck at a desk in Washington for the next ten years. And by then it would be over."

"What would be over?"

"What's happening in Poland."

She wasn't sure if she wanted to know what was happening in Poland. From what he had told her at the Czech restaurant she knew that Poland had a lot of foreign debt, but she didn't know much else since she didn't read the newspaper. But feeling it would be rude not to pursue this line of conversation, she asked: "What's happening there?"

"You don't know?"

"I haven't been following the situation."

"Well, come and sit down and I'll tell you about it. Would you like a brandy?"

"I don't know. I really don't like the taste of it."

"How about a blackberry brandy?"

She remembered taking sips of that after family meals, and she had liked it. "All right. But please don't give me a lot."

While he went into the kitchen she explored the living room. On the wall opposite the Polish coat of arms was a framed photograph of a woman. She had dark hair and dark eyes, and she was beautiful. The photograph was signed: "Kalina."

She concluded that the woman wasn't a girlfriend. For one thing, the photograph was black and white, and it must have been taken years ago. And for another thing, the woman looked like Marek. She had the same eyes, with the same bottomless need in them. The woman had to be his mother.

Not wanting Marek to catch her in front of the photograph, Eva went to the sofa, where she sat down and looked at a book on the coffee table. It was a book on the modern art of Poland. She lifted the cover and started leafing through it just to be doing something when he returned.

"Here," he said, handing her a small crystal glass that was half filled. He had a snifter of brandy in his other hand. "*Na zdrowie.*"

"*Na zdrowie.*" The sweet taste of the blackberry brandy stirred memories that saddened her.

Marek sat down next to her but not too close. He began to tell her what was happening in Poland, focusing on the rise of Solidarity and the emergence of Lech Wałęsa as the leader of a movement that might enable Poland to regain its independence. He also talked about the pope's support of this movement.

"Are you a Catholic?" she asked him at that point.

"No. I'm an atheist," he told her. "But I appreciate the value of the pope's support."

"Were you raised as a Catholic?"

"Of course I was. But I liberated myself from religion."

"Well, I don't see how anyone can be an atheist. You can't prove that God doesn't exist."

"You can't prove that He does exist."

"I don't have to. I know He exists."

"So let's agree to differ on that. I won't try to talk you out of believing in God, and you won't try to talk me into believing in Him. Okay?"

"Okay." But she still didn't see how anyone could be an atheist.

As he continued talking about Poland, her eyes wandered over to the photograph of the woman who she believed was his mother. Finally, having heard enough about Poland, she asked: "Is that your mother?"

It took him a long moment to respond. "Yes. That's her."

"What happened to her?"

"How do you know something happened to her?"

"I don't know. I just have a feeling."

"Well, your feeling is right." He stopped there, and for a long time he didn't say anything.

She waited, hoping he would tell her without prompting.

"Do you really want to know?"

"If I didn't," she said, "I wouldn't have asked."

"All right," he said. "I'll tell you."

She waited again.

"My mother was an actress. Her stage name was Kalina. I didn't know her real name until only a few years ago, but it doesn't matter. She acted on the stage, and she had minor parts in some of the films directed by Wajda. I assume you know Andrzej Wajda."

"No. I'm sorry. I never saw a Polish film. I saw *Rosemary's Baby* by Roman Polanski, but that's not a Polish film. And I didn't like it."

"You're right. It wasn't a Polish film. And it was trash. But before Polanski sold out to Hollywood he made some good films—the ones he made in Poland. My mother had a minor part in one of them."

"What was she like?"

"I never knew her. She abandoned me a few weeks after I was born, and she never came back."

"Never?" she said, her heart going out to him.

"Never," he repeated forlornly.

"How could she have done that?"

"I don't know, but she did."

The stark knowledge of his being abandoned by his mother sent a wave of sympathy through her and brought tears to her eyes. "Who raised you?"

"My father did. His sister, my aunt, helped him. But he mainly did it on his own."

"So your mother never came back to see you?"

"No. Never. She stayed away and pursued her career."

"Did you ever try to find her?

"On my first trip to Poland for the bank I tried to find her. There wasn't much of a trail because she hadn't been in a film for a while, and people didn't remember her. But on my third trip I found someone who knew her, someone who knew what happened to her." He paused, with a look of an unutterable despair in his dark eyes. "On her fortieth birthday she filled a bathtub, climbed into it, and slit her wrists."

"Oh, God," she said, clapping her hand to her mouth.

There was a long, long silence, and then he said: "It happened after my first trip to Poland, so she might have heard I was looking for her. It made me feel like she didn't want to see me, like she would rather die than see me."

"Maybe she didn't want to face you."

He shook his head. "If she had any regrets about abandoning me, she would have wanted to see me—to make amends. But she didn't want to see me. She didn't even want to know what had become of me."

"How old was she when you were born?"

"She was eighteen. And she didn't want to have a baby. I was an accident."

Eva reached out and took his hand. "You weren't an accident. You were part of God's plan."

"You agreed not to try to talk me into believing in God."

This injunction didn't leave her with many alternative ways of comforting him. In fact, there seemed to be only one way. She took him into her arms and held him, kissing his head and stroking his back.

A few minutes later their mouths came together, and they entered a realm where even though she couldn't prove that God existed, she could prove that she loved him.

Eva was in the kitchen making a chicken dish from her Polish cookbook when Marek got home. She didn't turn from the stove to greet him.

"That smells good," he said, softly kissing the side of her neck. "What is it?"

"*Kurczaka z pieczarkami.*"

"They smell like wild mushrooms."

"They are. They're dried mushrooms from Italy."

"I'll bring you some dried mushrooms from Poland the next time I go there." He went to the refrigerator and got out the bottle of vodka. "Would you like a shot?"

"No, thanks."

"Is something wrong?"

"Yes," she said, turning from the stove and facing him. "I smelled perfume in our bed. And it wasn't mine."

He laughed in relief. "Oh, that was Nadzia."

"What was she doing in our bed?"

"Taking a nap. She was kicked out of her flat last night. She called me at the bank, and I called you to ask you to let her in, but you didn't answer."

"What time was that?"

"Around three."

"I was over at the Wallace. So you came here and let her in?"

He nodded. "Yes. I left her here and went back to work."

"What if I'd come home and found her here?"

"You saw her before," he said with a shrug. "You know who she is. So there wouldn't have been a problem."

"You mean," she said, speaking slowly, one word at a time, "I would have come home and found a woman sleeping in our bed and there wouldn't have been a problem?"

"Why would there have been a problem?"

"I might have wondered what was going on."

"But nothing's going on. She's only a student from Poland who needs my help."

"So why don't the boys help her?"

"They do help her. But today she couldn't reach them. They don't have telephones."

"Why wasn't she here when I got home?"

"I found a place for her to stay, so I called her and told her to go and check it out."

"When did you call her?"

"Around four."

"Then I could have met her coming down the stairs."

"You could have. And she would have told you I let her take a nap in our apartment."

"Can I assume," Eva asked after processing what he had told her, "that she won't have to come here again and take a nap?"

"I think you can. She still needs my help, but at least she has a place to sleep."

"What does she do? I mean for a living?"

"She works in kitchens, she takes care of children, she does whatever work she can find."

"What did she do in Poland?"

"She was a student leader. They arrested her and held her for a while, but then they released her. And she decided to get out of Poland before they changed their minds."

"Do they usually release the people they arrest?"

He shook his head. "They usually don't."

"Then she was lucky."

"Yes. She was."

"All right," Eva said, believing his story. She understood why he was helping that woman, though she didn't have the sympathy for Nadzia that she had for Lukasz and Czeslaw. And she still had a feeling that the secret police had sent her to stop Marek from accomplishing his mission. "But I think you should be careful with her."

"I am being careful with her," Marek insisted. "I haven't told her anything about what I'm doing in Poland."

"Then what do you talk about with her?"

"Nothing. I'm just helping her get settled in London." He poured a shot of vodka, gulped it down, and refilled his glass. "Do you think I'm having an affair with her?"

"Well, any wife would wonder if she smelled another woman's perfume in her bed."

"So now you know why she was here," he said, putting the bottle back into the refrigerator, "and you don't have to wonder. But what if I *was* having an affair with her?"

"You asked me that question before."

"I know. I'm asking it again."

"And I'm telling you again that you don't have to test me. You know I love you."

"How do I know you love me?"

"I've proven it. I've stood by you. I've moved halfway around the world with you. I've suspended my career for you. And I believe you," she added for good measure, "when you tell me that woman only took a nap in our bed."

"So you trust me."

"Completely."

"I wish I had your faith," he said, gazing at her in wonder.

As she lay awake that night thinking about it, her faith was reinforced by her reason. If Marek were having an affair with Nadzia, he wouldn't have brought her to their apartment to have sex. He would have assumed that his wife was there, and if she was out, he would have known that she could walk in at any time. So he must have told her the truth about what Nadzia was doing in their bed.

The next day her mother called and gave her the bad news about her father. The tests had confirmed that he had cancer, and it was at an advanced stage. The doctors didn't expect him to live for more than six months.

That evening she and Marek agreed that she should book a flight home on Sunday, when he was planning to go to Poland, so they would be away at the same time.

A few days later she met Juliana for lunch in a restaurant that had recently become popular with merchant bankers.

As usual the head waiter seated them at a table where Juliana was on display, and the dark-suited men who passed their table circumspectly paid tribute to her.

After they had ordered, Eva said: "My father has cancer."

"Oh, no." Juliana instinctively reached across the table and found her hand. "What kind of cancer?"

"Lung cancer. They give him less than six months to live."

"I'm so sorry," Juliana said directly from her heart.

"I'm going home on Sunday."

"For how long?"

"A week. My classes start the week after next."

"You could miss some classes."

"I know I could. But I want to be here when my husband gets back from Poland."

"Your husband can take care of himself."

"I know, but—" She hesitated, wondering if she should tell Juliana about the perfume.

"What is it?" Juliana asked as if she detected something.

"It's that woman who called and wouldn't leave a message. I saw her with Marek on the street, and a few days ago he brought her to our apartment and let her take a nap there."

"He let her take a nap in your apartment?"

"She hadn't slept the night before."

"Well, that was nice of him," Juliana said with a hint of irony.

"I know how it sounds," Eva said. "And I admit that I had suspicions when I smelled her perfume in our bed."

"You smelled her perfume in your bed?"

"Yes. So I asked him about it, and he explained why she was there. And I believed him."

"Most women wouldn't have believed him."

"I know, but think about it. If he was having an affair with that woman, he wouldn't bring her to our apartment."

"No. He wouldn't. Unless he wanted you to catch him," Juliana added after a moment.

"Why would he have wanted me to catch him?"

"I don't know. I don't know him that well. But there are men who have to test the women who love them."

"Did a man ever do that to you?"

"No. But the father in the family I lived with in New York did it to the mother. He even tried to use me for that purpose."

"Well, my husband doesn't have to test me," Eva affirmed. "He knows I love him."

"Then you don't have to worry about that woman."

"Yeah, I do. I still have a feeling that the people who don't like what he's doing in Poland sent her here to lure him into a situation where they could harm him."

"Have you told him about your feeling?"

"I have. But he told me not to worry. He said she escaped from those people, so she wouldn't do anything for them."

"And you still worry about her?"

"I do. I don't know why."

"Well, remember what I said before," Juliana said. "It doesn't do any good to worry."

"I know it doesn't," Eva said. "And I have something more important on my mind."

"You do. I'll pray for your father."

"Thank you. He needs it."

On her way home she stopped at St. James and prayed in the Lady Chapel. She asked the Blessed Mother to make her father's cancer go away. She offered to forgive her father for what he had done to her mother. She promised to love her father as she had before she saw him go into that hotel. She focused her whole mind on her father.

After leaving the church she went to the market and bought groceries, intending to channel her energy into making dinner for her husband: pork chops, potatoes, and green beans.

Passing a corner newsstand, she was jolted by the headlines of a tabloid, which read: "POLISH STUDENT EXECUTED."

Inside she learned that it was Czeslaw.

EIGHT

MAREK WANTED HER to spend the night with him, but she didn't want Ramona to worry, and also she needed time to assimilate what she had done, so he walked her home and up the stairs of her building and kissed her goodnight before she closed the door behind her.

It was almost two in the morning, but Ramona was waiting up for her, lying on the sofa in her nightgown with an opened magazine resting on her chest.

"Are you all right?" Ramona asked, sitting up.

"I'm fine," Eva told her. "I'm sorry if I made you worry."

By now Ramona was on her feet and coming toward her, searching her face, and Eva knew she couldn't hide it from her friend. In fact, she didn't want to hide it.

"Oh, my God," Ramona said, evidently guessing what had happened. She put her arms around Eva and held her.

Eva pressed her face against Ramona's shoulder, not wanting to face what she had done. She finally pulled her head back and said: "I had sex with him."

"It's all right. Things happen."

"But what if he doesn't love me? What if he doesn't want to marry me?"

"If he doesn't, then you certainly don't want to marry him."

"But I have to now."

"No, you don't. You don't have to marry a guy just because you had sex with him."

"If I don't, then I've committed a sin."

"You've committed a sin anyway. But sins can be forgiven. Marriages can't be forgiven." Ramona guided her toward the sofa, saying: "Come and sit down."

They sat down next to each other.

She turned to Ramona and began to tell her what had happened. "We had dinner at a Hungarian restaurant, and then he asked me to go to his apartment, like you said he would. His apartment was only a block away."

Ramona didn't have to say: "So he must have planned it."

"On one wall of his apartment was a banner with the Polish coat of arms, and on another wall was a photograph of a beautiful woman. I could tell it was his mother."

"How could you tell?"

"She looked like him. And he confirmed it. She was an actress. She was in a film by a famous Polish director."

"Roman Polanski?"

"No, someone I never heard of. His mother got pregnant, and she didn't want to have a baby, so she abandoned him to pursue her career."

"And you felt sorry for him."

"Well, imagine being abandoned by your mother."

"It would be painful," Ramona acknowledged. "But why did he tell you about it?"

"I asked him what happened to her."

"What made you think something happened to her?"

"The first time I had dinner with him he talked about his father, but he didn't say a word about his mother. I thought it was strange, so I asked him about her. And he stared at me like he didn't know what the word meant."

"What made you ask him about her again?"

"It was seeing her photograph."

"I think it's strange that he displays her photograph. I mean, if his experience was so painful, why would he want to remind himself of it?"

"I don't know. Maybe deep down he loves her."

"How could he love her after what she did to him?"

"Maybe he can't help it. After all, she was his mother."

Ramona frowned. "So what happened to her?"

"On her fortieth birthday," Eva said, "she killed herself by slitting her wrists."

"Madre de Dios," Ramona said.

"He thinks she knew he was looking for her and didn't want to see him."

"So she killed herself to avoid seeing him?"

"That's what he thinks."

Ramona shook her head. "That doesn't make sense. It would make sense if she killed herself because she was depressed, or because she turned forty and hadn't succeeded in her career, but not because she didn't want to see her son."

"Well, it doesn't matter why she killed herself. What matters is how it made him feel."

"And how did it make *you* feel?"

"It made me feel sorry for him. It also made me feel I could help him. He told me he was an accident, and I told him he wasn't an accident, he was part of God's plan. He told me he didn't believe in God, so—"

"You offered yourself in place of God."

"I didn't presume to do that. I only wanted to prove to him that someone loved him."

"Then you offered yourself in place of his mother."

"I guess I did," Eva said, reflecting.

"I hope you don't think you can take her place."

"I know I can't. But I think I can make him stop feeling lost because of what she did to him."

"Only you can save me," Ramona said sardonically.

"I know you think it was only a line to get me to have sex with him, but I don't think it was."

"Do you have another date with him?"

"No. As a matter of fact, he didn't say he would call me. He only said goodnight."

"He could have meant goodbye. He got what he wanted. At least you don't have any risk of getting pregnant."

She had finished her period two days ago, as Ramona knew because they were more or less in sync. But even without the fear of getting pregnant Eva had enough other fears to keep her awake when she finally went to bed.

She waited a week for Marek to call her. During that time she didn't sleep well, and she couldn't focus on her work. She began to wonder if Ramona was right in believing that from his opening line Marek had only wanted to have sex with her. She began to wonder if he had hung that photograph on the wall to prompt her to ask him about his mother, and even if he had made up the story about his mother.

At the first opportunity she went to St. Jean Baptiste and confessed what she had done, and she did penance far beyond what the priest instructed, but Marek's failure to call her was worse than any punishment the church could have devised for her.

She went into a chapel and knelt and prayed to St. Thérèse: "O Little Flower of Jesus, you have shown yourself so powerful in your intercession, so tender and compassionate toward those who honor you and invoke you in suffering and distress, that I kneel at your feet with perfect confidence and beseech you most humbly and earnestly to take me under your protection in my present necessity and to obtain for me this favor I ask—that Marek call me. Recommend my request to Mary, the merciful Queen of Heaven, that she may plead my cause at the throne of Jesus, her divine Son. Intercede for me until my request is granted. Pray for me. Amen."

She waited two more days for her prayer to be answered, and finally since she couldn't bear it any longer, she called Marek. Again, she got a secretary and left a message and waited for him to call her back.

He didn't call her until that evening.

Ramona answered the phone, and holding her hand over the mouthpiece said: "It's him."

Eva rushed to the phone with her heart pounding.

From her friend's lips she read the phrase: *"Hijo de puta."*

"Hello?" she barely managed to say.

"Witam. To Marek. Jak się masz?"

"I'm fine. How are you?"

"Could you meet me somewhere for a drink?"

"Where?" If he asked her to go to his apartment, she would refuse. At least she hoped she would.

"There's a bar on Second Avenue where we could have a private conversation." He gave her its name and location.

"Okay. When?"

"I'll be there in ten minutes."

"I'll see you then."

While she changed her clothes and fixed her hair Ramona followed her around giving her advice. "Make him explain why he didn't call you, don't let him feed you another line, and don't go to his apartment."

"I will, I won't, I won't," she agreed.

He was sitting at the bar when she got there, and he led her to a table in the corner.

She had hoped that he would look happy to see her, and that he would hug her, but he kept his distance from her as if he didn't want her to catch a contagious disease.

When she was seated he went back to the bar and got her a white wine, which he set down on the table carefully.

"Why didn't you call me?" she asked.

He gave her a long sorrowful look with his dark eyes, and then he said: "I decided it would be better for you not to get involved with me."

"Why didn't you decide that before we had sex?"

"It wasn't my idea, it was yours."

"I started it," she admitted, "but you went along with it."

"I know. And I was sorry. I should have stopped when I realized it was your first time."

"You were sorry you had sex with me?"

"I was sorry I got you involved with me."

"Well, I wasn't sorry—until you didn't call me. And then I began to wonder if my roommate was right about you."

"What did she say?"

"She said you were only giving me a line to get me to have sex with you."

He shook his head. "I wasn't giving you a line. And I had no intention of having sex with you until it happened. Believe me."

"Why should I believe you?"

"Because everything I told you is true."

"What you told me about your mother is true?"

"Yes. Why would I have made up something like that?"

"To make me feel sorry for you."

"I don't want you to feel sorry for me."

"What do you want me to feel?"

"I don't want you to feel anything for me."

"Why not? Are you afraid of me?"

"I'm afraid *for* you." He took a long deep breath, and then with apparent difficulty he said: "Everything I told you is true. But I haven't told you everything."

"Then you should," she said, meeting his gaze.

"I really shouldn't. I promised not to tell anyone. But it wouldn't be fair not to tell you. So I'm going to tell you, but you have to promise not to tell anyone."

"I promise not to tell anyone."

"That includes your roommate, your mother, and your father. You can't tell anyone."

"I won't tell anyone, but will you explain why not?"

"Because if you did, it could get me killed."

She remembered what Ramona had said about not letting him feed her another line, and this was beginning to sound like a line, but she suspended her judgment, wanting to give him the benefit of a doubt. "All right. That's a good reason."

After glancing around to make sure that no one was listening, he said in a low voice: "It's true that I work for a bank. But it's only a cover. I really work for the CIA."

"You work for the CIA?" she was going to exclaim when he reached out and put the tips of his fingers to her mouth.

"Be careful. They could be listening."

"All right," she said, lowering her voice. "What do you do for that organization?"

"I collect information from Poland. I go there ostensibly to talk about the government's foreign debt, but my real purpose is to collect information on what's happening there. We have a source that's close to Jaruzelski."

"I don't know much about Polish politics. Who's Jaruzelski?"

"He's the prime minister of Poland, a military man, a Russian puppet, and a traitor," Marek said with contempt.

"So what's your mission?"

"It's to liberate Poland from the Russians."

"My father would support that. It's all he talks about with his friends—liberating Poland from the Russians and establishing a democratic government."

Marek nodded approvingly. "Your father has the right idea. What does he do for a living?"

"He works in a factory."

"Does he belong to a union?"

"Oh, yes. My father's always been active in the union."

"Then he would appreciate what's happening with the unions in Poland. There's an underground union movement that was organized by Bogdan Borusewicz, Andrzej Gwiazda, Krzysztof Wyszkowski, and several others. It was joined about two years ago by a man named Lech Wałęsa, who was involved in the strikes at the Gdańsk Shipyard. He could be the leader of a movement that overthrows the government."

"How would they do that?"

"Peacefully. They're against violence."

"Then they must have the support of the pope."

"They do. The pope is a key factor in what's happening there."

Eva smiled. "So even though you're an atheist you like having the pope's support."

"I don't care who supports us if they help us liberate our country. And I don't have anything against the pope. In fact, I admire him. I just don't share his religious beliefs."

"All right," she said after a silence. "I know you work for—that organization. But I don't know why you think it would be better for me not to get involved with you."

"My life," he explained, "is always at risk. On my next trip to Poland they could arrest me, they could torture me, and they could kill me."

"Well, women marry cops and firemen and soldiers whose lives are always at risk."

"They do, but eventually they must regret it."

"Not if they love the men they married."

"Sooner or later their love must get tested."

"I'm sure it does. And I'm not saying that all their marriages survive. But if I married a man whose life was always at risk, my love for him would pass any test."

"Would it pass the test of always worrying about him?"

"With God's help, it would," she said with blind confidence.

"Would you pray for your husband?"

"Yes. I would. I'd ask the Blessed Mother to protect him."

"What if she didn't? Would you lose your faith?"

"I hope I wouldn't," Eva said. "I hope I'd understand that it was God's will."

"What if your husband killed someone?"

"You mean in the line of duty?"

"Yes. Would you still love him?"

"I'd love him no matter what he did."

Marek leaned toward her. "What if he betrayed you?"

"What do you mean?" she asked, feeling the return of a sharp pain from an old wound.

"What if he cheated on you?"

"I would be hurt."

"How hurt?"

"Extremely hurt. But I'd still love him."

"You would?" he asked skeptically. "How could you love a man who cheated on you?"

"I told you," she said. "I'd love him no matter what he did. But I'd expect him to be faithful to me."

"You mean you'd trust him."

"I'd trust him completely."

"You know," he said after a silence, "by telling you who I really work for, I've put my life into your hands. So I'm trusting you completely."

"I know. And I'm glad you told me."

"I guess I should have told you before."

"It wouldn't have changed things."

He finally looked happy, and he didn't surprise her by asking: "Will you marry me?"

"Do you love me?"

"I love you more than you love your God."

"Well, that's nice, but just remember— I'm only a flawed human being."

"As far as I'm concerned, you're absolutely perfect."

"I'm not perfect, and I know you're not. But I love you, and I always will. So of course I'll marry you. But you have to meet my family and get their approval."

"Then let's go to St. Paul," he said, full of exuberance.

When he asked her to go to his apartment she declined, telling him she thought they should wait until they were married.

Marek spent the next week cutting through the red tape that prevented them from sending Czeslaw's body back to Poland so that his family could bury him there. First he had to get the body released from the police, who were investigating the murder, and then he had to clear the shipment through the respective governments. He finally received clearance from the Polish government through the influence of his bank.

They held a memorial service for Czeslaw at the Polish church in Balham that he attended, Kosciol Chrystusa Krola. Czeslaw had been a devout Catholic, and his commitment to the cause of liberating Poland had been as much religious as political. Like so many others he opposed communism not only because it was Russian but also because it was atheistic.

Eva had never heard Czeslaw and Marek argue about religion, presumably because they were bonded by their common cause, but she could imagine their difference becoming important if they succeeded in liberating their country. Now they would never have a chance to argue about religion, and as if he were conscious of this lost opportunity Marek paid his respects to Czeslaw by participating in the service even to the point of blessing himself when the priest said: *"W imię Ojca, i Syna, i Ducha Święte."*

On the same day that Czeslaw's body was shipped to Poland, Eva boarded a flight for New York, where she would connect with a flight to St. Paul. During most of the long transatlantic flight she stared out the window into the empty sky and thought about Czeslaw. Though they were about the same age, she had felt like a mother toward him, and she was overwhelmed by the thought of how his real mother would feel when his body arrived in Poland. With tears in her eyes and sorrow in her heart she asked God: "Why did You let them kill that boy? What purpose is being served by his death?"

Her questions were different from the practical questions that Marek and Lukasz had asked in their endless sessions of analysis following the execution of their friend. Who had killed him? How had they known he was involved in a plot to overthrow the government? How had they known where to find him?

Their questions should have been easier to answer than hers, but they were just as baffled as she was. All they were sure of was that whoever killed Czeslaw was also responsible for telling the government about the arms shipments.

Of course she worried more than ever about Marek's safety. If they could kill Czeslaw, they could kill Marek, and they had more reason to kill Marek since he was the leader. But maybe they were afraid to kill a member of the CIA. Or maybe they were using him to keep track of what the opposition was doing. In any case, she would have preferred Marek to have some other kind of job and not to be involved in Poland, except as a banker. But Marek had warned her not to get involved with him, and in marrying him she had accepted the fact that his life would always be at risk, so she couldn't complain about the situation.

Her mother met her at the airport. She had seen her mother in early January before she moved to London, eight months ago, but it seemed like eight years ago. In a long hug she shared with her mother her feelings about her father's illness without having to put them into words, but she couldn't share with her mother her feelings about what had happened in London. They no longer lived in the same world.

"How's Papa?" she asked her mother as they drove away from the airport.

"He's not doing well," her mother said. "I'm glad you came to see him now."

"You mean he doesn't have much longer?"

"The doctors give him a few months."

She found her father in the living room, seated in a lounge chair. His face was hollow, and his eyes were even more deeply sunk into their sockets than she remembered. The stubble on his cheeks and chin was flecked with silver.

At the sight of him, reduced to a shell of what he had been, it no longer mattered to her that he had cheated on her mother. It wasn't for her to judge her father.

She put her arms around him and hugged him.

"*Jak to moja polska dziewczynka?*" he asked.

"Your Polish girl is fine," she said. "How are you?"

"I'm not so good. But I'd feel better if I had a cigarette."

She glanced at her mother, who nodded, indicating that it wouldn't make any difference now. She found a pack of cigarettes on a side table and handed it to him. She watched his trembling fingers tweeze a cigarette out of the pack.

"Can you give me a light?"

"Yeah. Sure." She found a lighter on the same table and lit his cigarette.

He inhaled deeply, closing his eyes, and then he said: "That's better. Now, tell me about your life in London."

"I'll go and start dinner," her mother said, leaving them alone.

She pulled up a chair and sat down near her father. She knew he wanted to hear about Marek, who was her only reason for being in London and her only life there. She also believed that her marrying Marek was the only thing she had ever done that had made her father happy. So she began to talk about what Marek was doing.

While she described what he was doing as a banker, it occurred to her that she could safely tell her father what he was really doing. That would make him happy.

"If I tell you something, will you promise not to tell anyone?"

"Something about Marek?"

"Yes," she said. "But you have to promise not to brag about it to your friends."

"I promise," he agreed, exhaling smoke.

"Well, Marek's job with the bank is just a cover. He really works for the CIA."

"The CIA? Really?"

"They have a source of information close to Jaruzelski—"

"That son of a bitch. He's a Russian stooge."

"Yeah, that's what Marek says."

"So what's Marek doing about him?"

"He's plotting to overthrow him." She explained how they were planning a demonstration of ten million people, and how they were trying to build an army to protect their leaders.

Her father listened as she told him what she knew about the plot, and when she finished, his eyes were shining with a hopeful light. It was as if he could now see a future for the country he had been forced to leave as a young man. With the hand that wasn't holding the cigarette, he reached out and took her hand, saying: *"Niech Bóg mu błogosław."*

Though the blessing he invoked was for her husband, she felt it also applied to her.

While she was helping in the kitchen after dinner, her mother said: "Whatever you told your father made him happy."

"I thought it would," she said, appreciating the confirmation.

"I won't ask you what it was, but I assume it wasn't that he's going to have a grandson."

"If it was that, I would have told you first."

Her mother sighed. "So he won't live to see a grandson."

"I hope you don't blame me for not yet having a baby."

"Not at all. You aren't married even a year."

"How long were you married when you had me?"

"Ten months. But things were different then."

"I'm not on the pill if that's what you mean."

"I didn't think you were. I know you're a good Catholic."

"So I did expect to be pregnant by now."

"Don't worry. It'll happen sooner or later."

"Si Dios quiere," she murmured.

"What does that mean?"

"God willing. It's Spanish. I learned it from Ramona."

"Bóg pozwoli," her mother said in Polish.

She was relieved that her mother understood that the timing of a grandson was out of her hands, and that she wasn't expected to produce one for her father to see. It would have been a blessing, but it wasn't her fault that it wouldn't happen.

When she returned to London her husband was still in Poland, having extended his stay there. Feeling the need for company, she called Juliana, who invited her to join her for a concert at St. Mary's, the church she attended. St. Mary's was on Cadogan Street, near where Juliana lived, and on Sunday afternoon they were performing unaccompanied choral works by composers who had lived before Bach, which Juliana thought she would enjoy, though Eva would have gone to the concert no matter what they were performing.

Juliana was outside the church, waiting for her. They greeted each other with a kiss on both cheeks, and then they went in. Eva had gone to a morning mass at St. James, where she had prayed for her father, and she was in the mood to listen to religious music, but she wasn't prepared for what she heard. They began with works by renaissance composers, an Ave Maria, a Salve Regina, a Gloria, and a meditation, singing in pure, clear voices that came from their souls.

Eva's spirits were lifted by the music, and she was transported to a higher realm by the *Miserere* by Allegri.

"Miserere mei, Deus," they sang, expressing what she felt after seeing her father confront death. *"Miserere mei, Deus, secundum magnam misericordiam tuam."*

Responding to this prayer for forgiveness, Eva let the tears stream down her cheeks without trying to wipe them away, and she was washed clean of any remaining judgment of her father. She was absolved.

Her classes began the last week of September, and she was glad to see that Francis had decided to continue the program. They fell back into their routine of sharing a taxi after class, and they began to meet for coffee before class.

On a Saturday, about two weeks after classes began, a bomb exploded next to the Chelsea Barracks killing two people and injuring more than thirty others. The IRA claimed responsibility for the bomb, which must have been intended to kill soldiers in the barracks. When she read about it in the Sunday newspaper Eva immediately thought about Francis, and when they met for coffee before the next class she could tell from his eyes how he felt about it.

"I didn't know they were going to do it," he told her, "and I don't know who did it. But I feel responsible for not being able to talk them out of it."

"If you never met with the people who did it," she pointed out, "you never had a chance to talk them out of it."

"I don't know that I never met with them. I could have. And they all talk to each other. So I did have a chance to talk them out of it."

"But if they don't want to hear what you're saying, it's their responsibility."

"It's mine too. I failed to reach their hearts and minds."

"I don't understand them. I mean, what do they expect to accomplish by killing people?"

"They want the British army to retaliate."

"But they didn't kill any soldiers. They killed two civilians."

"So they won't get the response they wanted."

"Does that mean they'll try again?"

Francis nodded. "Unless someone can make them see that it won't get them anywhere."

She sipped her coffee, trying to make sense of a senseless action. "Why do they want the British army to retaliate?"

"It will give them a pretext for more violence. And of course they're hoping that the army will kill innocent people in trying to kill them. The more, the better."

"But why?" she asked, not following the logic.

"So the public will turn against the government."

"You mean they're willing to sacrifice innocent people to turn the public against the government?"

"Yes. They're willing to do anything for that purpose."

"But why do they have to sacrifice people? Why don't they try to convince the public that their cause is just?"

"That's a good question. They could respond that they tried using a nonviolent approach, and it didn't work because the public wouldn't listen."

"Is that true?"

"It's partly true. But there were some who always believed that violence is the only way."

"I guess it works in certain situations."

"It appears to work, at least for a while. But violence only leads to violence, so it's not the solution. It never is."

"What if a government is so oppressive that you don't have any alternative?"

"You always have an alternative."

She reflected for a while, and then she said: "You remember that Polish student who was killed a few weeks ago?"

"I do," Francis said. "I thought of you when I read about it."

"I knew him," Eva said. "I had him to dinner, and I cooked Polish food for him. I watched him eat it, feeling like his mother. He was just a boy."

"Imagine how his parents feel."

After a silence Eva said: "Well, you're a priest. Explain to me why God let them kill that boy."

"I can't explain it. I can only tell you that somehow it served God's purpose."

"But you can't explain how."

"I'm sorry. I can't."

"I know we're supposed to believe that whatever happens serves God's purpose, but sometimes I wonder."

"I do too. But then I remind myself that I'm only human, and that I can never understand why God does things. I can only accept what God does."

"My husband doesn't believe in God."

"What does he believe in?"

"Liberty and justice."

"Is he working to achieve them?"

"Yes. He is." She couldn't say any more than that.

"Then he's serving God's purpose. Liberty and justice come from God. All good things come from God."

"What about evil things?"

"They also come from God."

"Is violence evil?"

"I think it is."

"My husband thinks violence is justified when you're pursuing liberty and justice."

"The people who planted that bomb use the same justification. They're pursuing liberty and justice."

"But he wouldn't kill innocent people."

"Maybe he wouldn't kill them deliberately," Francis said, "but whenever you use violence you take the risk of killing innocent people. You've decided that achieving your goal is worth the sacrifice of human lives."

"I guess you have."

"And even if you tried to avoid killing innocent people, how would you identify them?"

"It wouldn't be easy."

"It wouldn't be possible. As human beings, we don't have the ability to decide who's innocent."

"Well, luckily my husband's only a banker," Eva said, feeling the need to cover for him, "so he doesn't have to deal with the issue of violence."

"We all have to deal with it," Francis said.

That evening, as she was climbing the stairs to their apartment, she smelled perfume. It was the same perfume that she had smelled in their bed.

She entered the apartment and stopped to listen, and she heard the rhythmic cry of a woman. With a churning stomach she went to the bedroom door and peered in.

The blond woman, naked, was straddling Marek, vigorously moving her buttocks up and down.

Marek was lying on his back, with his head resting on the pillow and his hands clasping the woman's waist, controlling the rhythm of her motion.

When he saw Eva, he raised his head slightly.

The woman stopped and turned her shoulders and looked at Eva insolently, and then as if she relished being in this situation, she swiveled back and resumed her motion at a faster rhythm and with louder cries.

Marek did nothing to stop her.

NINE

THE WEDDING WAS in early October. She would have liked to get married sooner, but her parents wanted a proper wedding at St. Casimir as well as a reception at the Polish-American Club, and the latter was booked through the end of the summer. She argued against the reception on the grounds that it would cost too much money, but her parents prevailed on the grounds that she was their only daughter, so it was the only reception they would ever have to pay for.

Eva introduced Marek to her parents on a trip to St. Paul in mid-July. Her father accepted Marek without any reservations, and in the evenings after dinner they sat on the deck and talked endlessly about the situation in Poland. Her mother did have some reservations, which arose mainly from not knowing Marek's family, and she asked a lot of questions about his father, about his mother, about his background. Eva gave her mother an expurgated version of Marek's story, but one question kept leading to another question, which made her feel that her mother was trying to get to the bottom of something.

"So his father raised him," her mother said as they were doing dishes on a typical evening, "and he never saw his mother."

"No. When he traveled to Poland he looked for her, but he never found her."

"That must have hurt him."

"It did. But he recovered from it."

"He evidently did. He has a good education, and he has a good job. But there's something about him that reminds me of your father."

"What do you mean?"

"I don't know. I guess it's that sad look in his eyes."

"Well, they both lost their country," she said, beginning to have an insight into her father.

"You're right. They're both exiles."

"But you lost your country, and you don't have that look in your eyes."

"I have a different way of dealing with it. They look back, and I look ahead. But at times I can't help looking back."

"I know what you mean. I couldn't wait to get out of here, but now at times I miss it."

"Then maybe you'll come and see us more often."

"I'm sorry. I was so busy with my job and going to school—"

"You don't have to explain. I understand."

She was relieved that her mother accepted her excuse for not coming home more often since she couldn't tell her mother the real reason. But now, with Marek out on the deck talking with her father, that reason wasn't so important. With Marek as her proxy she didn't have to deal directly with her father.

"You know," her mother said, "when you live with someone you have to live with what happened to him, and you have to understand that you can't change it."

"But you can help him live with it, can't you?"

"You can, up to a point. But there's a limit on what you can do for him."

"If you really love him, there shouldn't be a limit."

"There shouldn't be, but there is."

"Well, I'm going to do everything I can for him, and the more I love him, the more I can do."

"There's also a limit on how much you can love someone."

"I don't believe that. Is there a limit on how much you can love me?"

"That's different. I'm your mother."

"So only a mother can love someone unconditionally?"

"Even mothers fail at that. Look at what Marek's mother did."

"But there was something wrong with her."

"There's something wrong with all of us. As human beings, we're just not able to love someone unconditionally."

"I don't believe that."

"I know," her mother said as if she had known before this conversation. "And I don't want you to learn the hard way. When you marry Marek you'll promise to love him no matter what happens. But something will happen that tests your love and makes you realize your love has a limit."

"Did that happen to you?" she asked, not daring to look at her mother.

Her mother nodded. "It happened every day in little ways, and it happened once in a big way."

She waited for her mother to tell her.

"I can tell you now since it might help you. Almost two years ago I found out that your father was cheating on me."

"How did you find out?"

"From someone in our community. When you live in this community," her mother reminded her, "you can't do anything without someone finding out about it."

"How did you feel?"

"Hurt, angry, sad, betrayed."

"So what did you do?"

"I told your father that if he didn't stop it immediately, and if he ever did it again, I'd kick him out and lock the door and never let him in again."

"Would you really have done that?"

"I don't know. But that's what I told him."

"I assume he never did it again."

"As far as I know."

"Did you forgive him?"

"That's a good question. And that's how I learned that my love had a limit. I did forgive him eventually, but I knew I could forgive him only once."

"Only once? Jesus said we should forgive people seventy times seven times."

"I know, but I couldn't. For something like that I could forgive your father only once."

Since her mother knew about it, there was no reason for not telling her mother she had known about it. The damage had already been done. "I knew about it."

"How did you know?"

"I saw him going into a hotel with her."

"Why didn't you tell me?"

"I knew it would hurt you. And I didn't see what good it would do to tell you."

"Is that why you wanted to get out of here?"

"I couldn't face either of you, knowing what I did."

"You were right not to get involved in it," her mother said after a moment. "It wasn't your problem, it was our problem. And we were able to work it out."

She went to her mother and hugged her. "I'm sorry."

Her mother, who seemed to understand that she wasn't apologizing, she was telling her mother she felt bad for her, said: "So always remember, your love has a limit."

She went to St. Paul again a month later to make preparations for the wedding. She got her dress from a shop on Fifth Street favored by the rich people who lived on Crocus Hill. She argued against spending so much money for a dress she would wear only once, but her parents prevailed. She finally understood that at least in their community weddings weren't for the bride and groom, they were for the parents.

It was a beautiful fall day when her father walked her up the aisle in St. Casimir and handed her over to Marek. She had never seen her father look so happy. Before he turned to go and sit down he patted Marek on the shoulder, not only approving but also blessing the only man who deserved his daughter.

Ramona, after trying again the night before to talk her out of marrying Marek, was there to support her as the maid of honor.

Her parents didn't know that Marek was an atheist, and no one in the community, including the priest, would have guessed it from the way he went along with the wedding mass. In fact, his performance made her doubt that he really was an atheist.

In the exchange of vows they promised to love each other no matter what happened. Despite what her mother had told her, she believed that her love did not have a limit.

The reception at the Polish-American Club was a big event. There was Polish food, enough to feed two hundred people, and there was a famous polka band, which played the music that the community loved, including the songs of Bobby Vinton. She thought she would gag when they started playing "Blue Velvet," but instead she felt a pang of nostalgia.

For the first dance her father led her onto the floor, and the band played a Polish version of "Daddy's Little Girl." She was surprised by how well her father danced since she mainly remembered him standing on the sidelines talking with the men while the women danced with each other, but he glided her around the floor like a master.

When the dance ended her father held her at arm's length and gazed at her with admiration. *"Kocham cię, moja polska dziewczynka."*

"Kocham cię, papa," she told him.

Before going to St. Paul they had moved almost all her things into Marek's apartment, so when they returned to New York she only had to get a few remaining items at the apartment where she had lived with Ramona.

After growing up in a house with four males she didn't have much trouble living with a man, and when she had questions about what she should do as a wife she only had to ask herself what her mother would have done. Of course she was surprised by how often Marek wanted to have sex, and she wondered if her father had been like that. She finally asked her mother, who said her father had been very demanding.

They lived together in New York for just two months, which were interrupted by two trips to Poland that Marek had to make. While he was on the first trip, remembering what he had said about his life always being at risk, she went to St. Jean Baptiste every morning and prayed for his safe return.

She still went to mass every Sunday with Ramona, and they still had brunch together. They saw each other at work almost every day, but they didn't have much time to talk at the hospital, so having brunch gave them an opportunity to catch up. Ramona always asked how things were going with Marek, and Eva always said they were going well.

But things changed when he came home one evening and told her they were transferring him to London. He hadn't mentioned this possibility, so she wasn't at all prepared for it.

"London? Why London?"

"It's closer to Poland. And there's a Polish community there."

"You mean a community of exiles?"

"Some of them have been living there since World War II," he said, "but a lot of them went there in 1968. My father and I almost went there. We came here because he had a connection in the State Department."

"What would you do there?"

"I'd work in the bank. It has a branch there."

"And what would I do?"

"You can work there as a nurse."

"I'd have to get a permit."

"They'll give you one. They must need nurses."

"I hope so. I mean, I'll go wherever you go, but it would be nice if I could work. If I couldn't work, I don't know what I'd do with myself."

"Well, you could have a baby."

"Yeah. I could." Since they were having sex almost every day, she wondered why she hadn't gotten pregnant. They hadn't even been using the rhythm method.

"You'll like London."

"Why will I like it?"

"It's a great city."

"How do you know?"

"I stopped there on my last trip."

"Why did you stop there?"

"To make contacts with the Polish community."

"Was the transfer to London your idea?"

"They asked me what I thought about it."

"And what did you tell them?"

"I told them I thought it was a good idea. I could be a lot more effective there."

"All right," she said, being a good wife. "When do we leave?"

"As soon as we get our visas."

It took until early January to get their visas, and by then she was ready to go. She had resigned from her position at the hospital and had spent a week in St. Paul with her family, without Marek, who had to spend two weeks with his real employer in Langley, Virginia, preparing for his assignment in London.

The hardest thing was saying goodbye to Ramona.

They had dinner together at Ramona's favorite restaurant, up in the Barrio. They ate *cuchifritos* and rice and beans and fried plantains, and they drank several rounds of *piña colada*. The more they drank, the more often they burst into tears at the thought of being so far apart.

Before they said goodbye Ramona told her: "If anything happens, you can always come back and stay with me."

"You're not going to get a roommate?"

"No. I don't need the money, and I like having the apartment to myself."

"I'll keep that in mind."

She remembered her friend's offer now as she knelt in the Lady Chapel. She had fled the scene and sought refuge in St. James, where she asked God: "Why have you done this? How could you have hurt me this way?"

When she didn't find answers she realized that though she was asking the right questions, she wasn't asking the right person. She should have been asking Marek why he had done this, and how he could have hurt her this way. And she *would* ask him. But she needed time to recover from the shock of what she had witnessed in their bedroom.

She considered packing up and taking a plane to New York and staying with Ramona for a while so that she could decide what to do. But if she did that, she would be running away from the problem. She had to stay in London and face it.

Then she remembered what her mother had said about her love having a limit. Was this her limit? Was her love conditioned on her husband being faithful to her?

She thought about what her mother had done. Her mother had eventually forgiven her father, but she had given him an ultimatum, making it clear that her love for him did have a limit. Should she do that with Marek?

But what he had done to her wasn't the same as what her father had done to her mother, who had heard that her husband was cheating on her but hadn't actually seen it. Her mother hadn't seen a naked woman straddling her husband.

Marek knew she would be returning from her class around that time, yet he had brought that woman into their apartment and into their bed. Had he wanted her to catch him?

Juliana had suggested that possibility. So maybe her husband was testing her love. And she could understand why he might feel the need to test her. After being abandoned by his mother, he needed assurance that Eva would love him no matter what he did. He had been completely open about that before he asked her to marry him, and he had warned her.

So what he had done with that woman in their bed was only a test. It didn't mean anything.

But it still hurt her. And shouldn't he be held responsible for his actions no matter what had happened to him when he was a baby? He did have a choice whether or not to test her, and he could have chosen not to test her.

She didn't see how she could ever forgive him. But then she recalled how she had reminded her mother what Jesus had said about forgiving someone seventy times seven times. How little she had known then.

Still, if her mother was able to forgive her father, she should be able to forgive Marek. After all, she had promised to love him no matter what he did.

"Holy Mary," she prayed with her eyes fixed on the Blessed Mother, "please help me deal with this."

An hour later she found Marek in the living room sitting on the sofa with a bottle of vodka on the coffee table and a shot glass in his hand. The woman was evidently gone, but the smell of her perfume lingered in the air.

Eva stopped and faced him with folded arms. "Why did you do this? How could you have hurt me this way?"

"I didn't do it to hurt you," he said, gazing at her sadly.

"Then why did you do it?"

"I wanted to see if you'd still love me."

"I said I'd love you no matter what you did. But you didn't have to test me."

"I felt I had to. I couldn't help it."

"So you brought that whore into our apartment, into our bed, knowing I'd come home and catch you with her?"

"I didn't know when you'd come home."

"You knew. I come home at the same time after my classes."

"All right, all right. I wanted you to catch me with her."

"And what do you expect me to do now?"

"I expect you to leave me."

"You expect me to abandon you the way your mother did?"

He frowned at her. "You think I did it because of what my mother did to me?"

"I don't know how else to explain it."

"Why do you have to explain it?"

"Because I can't believe you'd hurt me for no reason."

"I didn't do it to hurt you," he repeated.

"But you did hurt me. You hurt me so much I almost can't bear it." Though she fought against them, tears began to flow from her eyes.

"I'm sorry," he said. "I'm really sorry."

"You should be. But I don't know if I can forgive you."

"I don't expect you to forgive me. In fact, I expect you to leave me and go back to New York."

"I seriously considered that. But I promised to love you no matter what happened."

"You didn't know what you were getting into."

"I should have known."

"You couldn't have known."

"Whatever I knew, I made a promise, and I'm not looking for an excuse to break it."

"Do you still love me?" he asked, appealing to her with the bottomless need that she couldn't help responding to.

"Yes," she said. "I still love you. But there's a condition, not on my love but on my willingness to live with you."

"What's the condition?"

"That you never, ever cheat on me again."

"I don't know if I can promise that."

"If you can't, then I'm packing up now and going back to New York."

"I think you should do that anyway—for your own good."

"We're not talking about my own good, we're talking about our marriage."

He sipped the vodka, reflecting. "All right. I promise never to cheat on you again."

"Then I'll stay with you."

A long way from kissing and making up, she left him in the living room and went into the bedroom, where she tore the sheets off the bed and stuffed them into a pillow case. She took the pillow case into the kitchen and set it down next to the garbage, intending to throw it out.

Then she went into the bathroom and got her bottle of spray cologne. From room to room, starting with the bedroom, she sprayed the air.

A week later Lukasz came to dinner with another student who looked like his younger brother. His name was Eryk, and he called her Pani Ostrowski until, not wanting to feel like his mother, she insisted that he call her Eva.

There had been some major developments in Poland. Wałęsa had consolidated his position as head of Solidarity, and Jaruzelski had announced on Sunday that he was assuming the role of first secretary of the communist party. He was already prime minister as well as defense minister, and his latest move confirmed the direction where he was heading.

"He's following the course of Stalin," Lukasz said as they sat in the living room discussing the situation. "His next move will be to establish a military government."

"We can stop him," Marek said. "There's another shipment of arms on the way, and we now have a potential force of about five thousand men."

"Five thousand against an army of three hundred thousand?" Eryk said.

"When they encounter armed resistance," Marek said, "the army will defect. They don't want to fight a war with their own people."

"But he could use Russian troops," Lukasz pointed out.

"He's not going to get them," Marek said. "He keeps asking for them, but they keep telling him it's not going to happen."

"I still don't understand their rationale," Lukasz said. "In the past the Russians have always sent troops to crush an uprising in Eastern Europe."

"Things have changed," Marek said. "The Russians need money, and if they invade Poland, the Western banks will cut them off."

"Couldn't they get money from the Middle East?"

"That money comes to London, and the banks here decide where it goes."

"Well, I hope we don't have another problem with the arms shipment," Lukasz said.

"I hope so too," Marek said.

At the dinner table she watched the two students pile their plates as if they hadn't eaten in days.

After dinner, while Marek was introducing Eryk to brandy, she took Lukasz aside and asked him: "Do you know Nadzia?"

"Yes," he said warily.

"How well do you know her?"

"Not very well. I met her through Marek."

"Do you know where she lives?"

"I helped her get settled."

"Could you give me her address?"

"I can't give you the number of her building, but I can tell you what street it's on, and the nearest cross street."

"That would be fine."

"Why do you want this information?"

"I have to talk with her about something."

"But couldn't you get her address from Marek?"

"It's something between her and me. He wouldn't understand."

"You mean it's a female thing?"

"That's right," she said truthfully.

He gave her the information, which she wrote down on a piece of note paper, not knowing what she was going to do with it.

A few days later Marek learned that the shipment of arms had been intercepted and that two of his contacts in Poland had been arrested.

"I don't know how they found out about it," he said, standing in the kitchen.

"Someone must have told them," she said, forgetting the dinner on the stove and giving him her full attention. She understood how vital the shipments of arms were.

"I know, but who?"

"Who knew about it?"

"Lukasz, Eryk, and two guys in Poland."

"Do you trust them completely?"

"Yes. I'm sure that none of them betrayed us."

"Either you're wrong about one of them, or someone else knew about the shipment."

"I'm not wrong about any of them."

"Then someone else knew about the shipment."

He stopped to think, and then he shook his head. "I can't think of anyone else."

"Did Nadzia know about it?"

"No. She didn't know about it."

"Are you sure you didn't tell her about it?"

"I'm sure I didn't," he said, bristling.

"Well, maybe somehow she found out about it."

"That's not likely. How could she have found out about it?"

"She could have seen your plan."

"I don't have a written plan."

"You must have something written on paper."

"I have notes, but she couldn't have seen them. They're in my briefcase, in a secret compartment."

"You never mentioned that before."

"I didn't want you to know about it."

"In case they tortured me to make me talk?"

"Don't joke about it," he said seriously.

"So anything written on paper is in your briefcase, in a secret compartment, which Nadzia doesn't know about."

"Why would I have told her and not you?"

She could imagine a few reasons, but she didn't believe them, so she didn't suggest them. She just said: "I don't know."

"I think you're on the wrong track," he said after a silence. "I mean, it's natural for you to suspect her after what happened, but one thing has nothing to do with the other."

"Maybe I am on the wrong track," she said. "But if you don't have a better idea, you should consider it."

"I will consider it. I have to consider every possibility. But how could she have found out where I keep my notes?"

"By snooping around. She had plenty of opportunity when you brought her here."

"I guess she did. She had access to my briefcase both times."

"What do you mean both times? I thought the first time you left her here to take a nap."

"I didn't," he admitted. "I stayed here with her."

"I don't need to hear the details," she said, fuming. "But while she was here—both times—she had an opportunity to find that secret compartment."

"She did. But I don't see a motive. After what they did to her, she wouldn't go over to their side."

"She would if they paid her enough money."

"No, she wouldn't. She's not a traitor."

"Whatever she is, you shouldn't trust her."

"From now on I won't," he agreed. "And I'll make sure she doesn't have access to any information."

Later that week she was informed that her nursing application had been accepted, and that the next step was to complete a program of orientation. Since she was in the middle of her course at Birkbeck, she scheduled the orientation for January, conscious of the fact that by then she wouldn't have worked as a nurse for a full year.

On Sunday her husband went to Poland in an effort to salvage the operation to put arms into the hands of the force that they had organized to protect the leaders of Solidarity.

While he was away two things happened. The IRA planted a bomb in a Wimpy Bar on Oxford Street that killed the police explosives officer who tried to defuse it. Since it happened on a Monday, she didn't have a chance to talk about it with Francis until the next day, when he took her to the Irish pub for dinner and blamed himself for failing to talk the IRA out of using violence. She did her best to comfort him.

She learned about the other thing while passing the newsstand on Blandford Street, where she noticed the headlines of a tabloid: "ANOTHER POLISH STUDENT KILLED."

She bought the paper, but she didn't have to read the story to know it was Lukasz.

TEN

AFTER LEARNING WHAT had happened, Marek caught the next flight back to London, and he immersed himself in the process of transferring his friend's body to Poland.

To avoid exposing members of their organization, Marek decided to have a small private memorial service for Lukasz instead of a public one, and to placate Eva he decided to stop having exiled student leaders come to dinner at their apartment. It was now clear that their key people were being systematically eliminated by the Russians, and that even in the relative safety of London they had to go underground.

Of course Eva worried that Marek would be next. If only by association with Czeslaw and Lukasz, the secret police knew that he was involved with the opposition, and sooner or later they would decide to eliminate him.

She expressed these feelings after they returned to their apartment from the memorial service. They were sitting on the sofa, exhausted.

"I don't want to go to another memorial service," she told him, staring into space.

"I don't either. I feel like I lost another brother."

"And what have you accomplished?"

"Nothing so far. But we still have a chance of stopping those bastards from establishing a military government."

"How can you stop them? They know what you're doing, and they keep stopping you."

"We have a new idea," he told her with a gleam in his eyes. "And they're not going to find out about it."

"What's the idea?" she asked, afraid.

"We're going to assassinate Jaruzelski."

"You're going to kill him?" She didn't like the idea. It was one thing to protect the leaders of Solidarity, but it was another thing to kill people, even people like Jaruzelski who had a lot of blood on his hands. "Whose idea was this?"

"It was my idea, but the person I report to supports it."

"Do the people higher up support it?"

"I assume they do or he wouldn't. But that's not my problem. My problem is to figure out how to do it."

"Well, I don't support it," Eva said. "I don't support the idea of killing people."

"They killed Czeslaw, and they killed Lukasz."

"That doesn't make it right to kill them."

"So we should let them kill us?"

"No. You have to defend yourselves."

"We do. And killing Jaruzelski is the most effective way of defending ourselves. If we get rid of him, they'll stop killing us."

"What if they don't? What if they kill more people because you killed him?"

"It's a risk we have to take. If you're not willing to risk your life for something," Marek added, "then you don't have a chance in hell of accomplishing it."

"But you're not only risking your own life, you're also risking other people's lives."

"They don't have to join us. They can stand on the sidelines."

"They can still get killed. That bomb near the Chelsea Barracks killed people who were standing on the sidelines."

"We're not going to use bombs. We're going to use a rifle to hit a specific target."

"I still don't support it. Why don't you go back to your idea of getting ten million people in the streets?"

"We haven't abandoned that idea. But we have to stop them from arresting our leaders. Without leaders we can't organize a demonstration. We can't mobilize the people."

"Are you going to try another arms shipment?"

He shook his head. "We don't have time. But we have some weapons we got from the army."

"How did you get them?"

"We bought them from the army. Those *pierdolony zdrajców* will do anything for money."

"Then why don't you pay them not to fight you?"

"We don't have that much money. So we have to assassinate Jaruzelski. If you want to immobilize an army, you cut off its head. That's standard doctrine."

"For the CIA, but not for the church. I know that the pope would never support your assassinating Jaruzelski."

"He should. They tried to assassinate him."

"If he supported violence, he wouldn't have any influence. And if Solidarity uses violence, it won't have any influence."

"Solidarity wouldn't be involved."

"But it would be blamed, wouldn't it?"

"No. The CIA would be blamed. It always is."

Lying in bed and thinking about this conversation, Eva resolved to keep trying to talk him out of using violence and to do whatever she could to protect him.

With the latter in mind, she walked the next morning to the Baker Street station and figured out from the tube map how to get to Balham. She took the Bakerloo Line to Elephant & Castle, and then changed to the Northern Line, which she took to the Balham station. She got directions from a newspaper vendor and easily found her way to the street where Nadzia lived. It was lined with townhouses, smaller than the ones in Marylebone.

Not knowing the number of the house, she had to watch the whole block in order to spot the woman. If she did spot her, she would follow her in the hope of getting evidence that Nadzia was the person who had betrayed them.

To avoid being recognized, she wore a jacket with a hood, which she pulled up over her head. It made her feel like a monk keeping vigil.

She loitered on the corner for more than an hour before she saw Nadzia come out of a house. At the sight of the woman who, straddling her husband, had given her that insolent look, she felt a wave of anger, but she contained it, turning her face to make sure that Nadzia wouldn't recognize her.

The woman walked past her, ignoring her, and headed for Balham High Road. Eva followed her to a pastry shop, where the woman sat down at a table and had a coffee and a croissant. Hoping that someone would join the woman, Eva lingered outside the shop as if she were waiting for the bus. By now she was cold, but she didn't want to risk going into the shop and having Nadzia recognize her.

After about a half hour the woman got up and came out. Avoiding eye contact, Eva advanced toward the street and stared at the cars going by. She waited a minute, and then she saw that Nadzia was heading back to her street.

At a safe distance she followed the woman back to where she lived. With disappointment she watched Nadzia go into the house. For all the time she had spent there, she had learned only the number of the house where Nadzia lived and the name of the place on Balham High Road where she had breakfast.

A few days later she had lunch with Juliana at the Portuguese restaurant on Beauchamp Street. Juliana was having a bout of homesickness that as usual made her seek the comfort food she had known in Brazil.

"If you're homesick," Eva said after they had ordered, "why don't you go home for a while?"

"If I went home," Juliana said, "my parents would worry about me. And they have three other children to worry about."

"You mean they'd worry that you'd do something to get into trouble with the military?"

"I don't have to do anything. I'm already in trouble with the military. I'm on their list. And they could stop me at immigration and arrest me."

"Are they likely to do that?"

"No, but they could."

"Then I guess you won't go home as long as the military are in power."

"I won't—unless something happens to my family."

"Well, I don't have to worry about being arrested," Eva said, "but I wouldn't have gone home unless something happened to my family, at least not for a while."

"How's your father?"

"He's dying."

"I'm sorry."

"But I'm glad I went. I made him happy."

"You mean by being there?"

"No. By giving him hope for Poland. I told him what my husband's doing there," Eva said carefully. "I knew it would make him happy. The only thing I ever did that made my father happy was marrying Marek."

"When I married Adrian, it made my father happy. It was like he could stop worrying about me."

"I guess we need our husbands to make our fathers happy."

"I guess we do."

"I never told you this," Eva said after a silence. "While I was at home before I got married, I learned that my mother knew my father had cheated on her."

"Our mothers always know more than we think."

"When she found out, she gave my father an ultimatum. She told him that if he didn't stop it, she'd kick him out and lock the door and never let him in again. And as far as she knew, he never cheated on her again."

"Did she forgive your father?"

"Yes. But she said she could forgive him only once."

"What about you? Have you forgiven him?"

"I think I have. At least I've stopped judging him."

"When people are dying," Juliana said, "it's a good time to stop judging them."

"I know. But what if they're not dying?"

Juliana looked at her. "Are you trying to tell me something?"

Eva hesitated, but she needed to tell someone about it, and Juliana might give her another perspective. "I caught Marek in our bed with a woman."

"You did? I'm sorry." Juliana reached out and took her hand. "But I have to tell you, I'm not surprised."

"I had a feeling you wouldn't be."

"When you told me about smelling perfume in your bed, I tried to warn you."

"I know you did. I should have listened to you."

"I didn't know if I was right. I mean, I wouldn't have believed it from any other man, but your husband's explanation for the perfume could have been true."

"It wasn't true. She didn't go to our apartment to take a nap. She went there to have sex with him."

"Well, I hope you gave him an ultimatum."

"I did. And I think he accepted it. At least he promised never to cheat on me again."

"So how do you feel?"

"I feel angry. But I understand why he did it."

"Why did he do it?"

"To test my love for him."

Juliana shook her head. "He has no right to do that."

"He has a need to do it," Eva said.

"He still has no right. A need to do something doesn't give you a right to do it, especially if you hurt someone."

"It did hurt me. But it didn't kill me."

"Then you passed the test?"

"I guess I did."

"Well, that might satisfy him for a while," Juliana said, "but he'll have the need again, and he'll test you again."

"I made it clear that if he cheats on me again, I'll leave him."

"But he could do something else to test you."

"I know he could." She made a decision. "My husband isn't really a banker. He works for the CIA."

"He does?"

"He's trying to overthrow the communist government in Poland. He's willing to kill for that purpose."

"When I belonged to a radical group, some of our members were willing to kill for our purpose."

"Were you?"

"No. I'm against killing for any purpose. I believe in the sanctity of human life."

"That's my position," Eva said.

"Then that's where he'll test you," Juliana said.

The waiter brought their food, and they began eating.

"You know," Juliana said, "you don't have to pass every test. It's not like getting a college degree."

"I know it's not."

"If you failed a test, there wouldn't be any consequences."

"There would be for him."

"What would happen to him?"

"He would be lost."

Juliana abruptly stopped eating. "I hope you don't believe you can save him."

"I believe I can."

"Well, you can't save him. You can save a person from drowning by pulling him out of the water, but you can't save a person from self-destructing by passing tests of your love for him. You simply can't do that."

"If God gives me the power, I can."

"Why should God give you the power?"

"To serve His purpose."

"If God gave anyone the power, He'd give it to your husband to save himself."

"I wish He would. I pray for it."

"Then maybe it'll happen. But if your husband tests you again, don't play the game."

"How do I know it's not God testing me?"

"God wouldn't test your love for your husband. He'd only test your love for Him."

"But we show our love for God by loving other people."

"I know we do, but there are people I can't love. I mean, I can't love people who want to torture me or kill me."

"You mean the generals who run Brazil."

"Yes. God loves them, but I can't."

"Beyond the generals, are there other people you can't love?"

Juliana considered. "I can't love people who want to hurt me or abuse me. I know I should, but I just can't."

"I thought I could. But now I wonder."

"Well, you don't have to prove you can. So stop trying."

The next week Marek returned to Poland, where he planned to stay as long as necessary. He believed that things were coming to a head, and he had decided to go ahead with organizing a demonstration of ten million people, while doing whatever he could to protect the leaders. At the same time he was going to pursue the idea of assassinating Jaruzelski. Before he left, Eva urged him to drop that idea, but he argued unconvincingly that the end justified the means.

While he was away she resumed her surveillance of Nadzia. She took the tube every morning to Balham, and she positioned herself on the street where she had a good view of the house where the woman lived, always with her hood pulled up.

She found that Nadzia had a routine of going out at the same time and having breakfast at the pastry shop and then returning to her apartment, where she remained for the rest of the day. Whatever she did outside of the house, she must have done in the evening. So after a few days Eva extended her vigil to the evening, when Nadzia finally went out again, no longer in jeans but now in a skirt, a very short one.

She followed the woman to the Balham tube station and from there to Green Park after changing at Stockwell to the Victoria Line. She stayed about twenty feet behind Nadzia, who walked down Piccadilly to White Horse Street, and up to Shepherd Market, where she stopped at a house and pressed the red-lit button near the door.

On a tour through the area with Juliana a few weeks after she arrived in London, Eva had learned the significance of the red-lit buttons in Shepherd Market, so as she watched the door open and let Nadzia in, she knew how the woman supported herself.

From that piece of information she concluded that she wasn't going to find out anything about Nadzia by watching her in the evenings, so she cut back the hours of her vigil.

After several mornings of tailing Nadzia to the pastry shop, she made a breakthrough. She was standing in the cold outside of the shop while the woman had her coffee and croissant when two large men in overcoats and hats went into the shop. They swaggered directly to the table where Nadzia was sitting, and they joined her there.

Since she might not have another opportunity like this, Eva had to take the risk that Nadzia would recognize her, so she went into the shop with her hood still up and stopped at the counter where the pastries were displayed.

"Can I help you?" a woman behind the counter said.

"What's inside those round things?" she asked, pointing to an unfamiliar pastry.

While the woman responded to her questions Eva tried to hear what the men were saying to Nadzia. They were speaking in Russian, which she could mostly understand.

"Do you have more information for us?"

"Not now," Nadzia said in what sounded like perfect Russian. "I don't have access to his briefcase anymore."

"Do you have any other sources of information?"

"Oh, yes. I have a lot of contacts in the Polish community."

"When would you like to meet again?"

"At the same time next week."

"All right." The man reached inside his overcoat and brought out an envelope. "This is for the information about the student leaders."

"Thanks," Nadzia said, taking the envelope, which she put into her pocketbook.

The men, who hadn't unbuttoned their coats or removed their hats, rose from the table and said: "*Do svidaniya.*"

"*Do svidaniya,*" Nadzia said.

Trembling with excitement, Eva ordered a pasty, which she asked the woman to wrap up, and she quickly left the shop.

Outside, she started walking in the opposite direction from the street where Nadzia lived, and when she had put a safe distance between her and the shop, she stopped to think. She had the information she had hoped to get, but now she didn't know what to do with it. Marek was in Poland, and unless he called her she had no way of giving it to him.

Nadzia couldn't do any more damage until next week, so Eva had time to think about it, and thinking about it led to a flurry of emotions. The woman was not only a whore, she was a *Russian* whore, and she had passed information that had led to the deaths of those dear boys and might lead to the death of Marek. The woman was a spy, pretending to be a Polish student, playing on the sympathies of people, and then betraying them. If anyone deserved to be killed, she did. And for a few moments Eva had the satisfaction of imagining herself with a gun in her hand, marching into the pastry shop and blasting that whore right in the face. For the Polish students who had been murdered by the Russians, she would strike a blow of justice.

Then she realized that though there would be justice in killing Nadzia, there would also be revenge, so she asked God to forgive her for having such murderous thoughts and to remove them from her mind. But somehow she had to find a way to stop Nadzia from doing more damage.

Marek was in Poland when Jaruzelski imposed martial law and established a military government. Though there were protests, they were crushed without the assistance of Russian troops. The leaders of the opposition were arrested, and at least a hundred people were killed, including some miners who went on strike at the Wujek coal mine.

Of course Eva worried that they would arrest Marek, and she waited anxiously to hear from him. She read the morning and evening newspapers, praying that she wouldn't see his name in them. As she followed the events she saw how the government had anticipated every move of the opposition and had brutally prevented it. She wondered how much the government owed its success to the information they had gotten from Nadzia.

She was in their apartment reading the evening newspaper when Marek came home. She ran to the door and hugged him, thanking God for his safe return.

He looked awful. He obviously hadn't shaved in days, and he probably hadn't slept in days. He dropped his luggage on the floor as if he would have no further use for it. In a low defeated voice he said: "I need a shot of vodka."

She got it for him and joined him on the sofa.

"*Stan wojenny, stan wojenny,*" he intoned, pouring a shot. "Our country's in a state of war, but it's a war against ourselves."

"The Russians never sent in troops?"

"No. It turned out that he didn't need them. He got help from your country."

"*My* country." She didn't understand. "What do you mean?"

"I found out who betrayed us. Guess who it was."

"I don't want to guess. Tell me."

"It was the organization I worked for."

"You mean the CIA?"

He nodded. "They didn't want an independent, democratic Poland. They wanted a military government. They wanted law and order. They wanted stability."

"You mean they helped Jaruzelski take over?"

"They told him about everything we planned to do. They told him about the arms shipments. They told him about our plan for a demonstration. They gave him the names of our leaders."

"How do you know?"

"They had the information, they had a motive, and they had the opportunity."

"But that doesn't prove they betrayed you," Eva argued. "Someone else could have done it."

"No one else had the information." He poured another shot of vodka. "I mean, no else who could have betrayed us had the information."

"Are you sure about that?"

"I'm absolutely sure. And the worst part is," Marek told her, giving her a look of infinite sorrow, "I worked for them. I helped those assholes betray my country."

"You don't work for them anymore?"

"No. I gave them a letter of resignation."

Wanting to relieve his pain, she made a decision. "Someone else had the information."

"Someone else? Who do you mean?"

"That woman you brought to our apartment."

"Oh, don't go into that again. I'm not in the mood."

"I have evidence that she betrayed you."

"I promised I wouldn't cheat on you again, and I haven't," he said heatedly. "So please don't confuse the issue by trying to get back at her."

"I'm not trying to get back at her. I'm trying to protect you."

"Protect me from what? Those *pierdolony zdrajców* have no reason for killing me now."

"They might have a reason. They might want to cover their tracks. They committed two murders here in London."

"Well, I don't know who did it."

"They might think you do."

"Why would they?"

"There's a connection between those murders and you."

"You mean Nadzia?" He looked at her impatiently. "All right. Tell me your theory."

"It's not a theory, it's a fact." She told him how she had watched the street where Nadzia lived, and how she had followed her to the pastry shop, and how she had followed her to Shepherd Market. "So I was right when I called her a whore."

"I didn't know she made a living that way."

She told him how she had finally seen Nadzia with the two Russian men in the pastry shop, and she told him what they had talked about.

"I didn't know she spoke Russian."

"She does. And she sounds like a Russian."

"She's Polish. But she's worse than a Russian. She's a traitor."

"Whatever she is, she promised to give those Russian men more information next week."

"I have to stop her," he said grimly. "A few of our leaders got away, and I have to protect them."

"What about you?"

"I don't need protection."

"But if you resigned from the CIA, who will protect you?"

"No one will protect me. No one ever did."

"Are you sure the CIA betrayed you?"

"Yeah. I'm sure. The person I report to told me the higher ups are happy with what happened."

"Why would they be happy?"

"The banks are happy. Banks don't like uncertainty."

"So they helped to establish a military government in Poland to give the banks a better chance of collecting their loans?"

"They evidently did."

"Well, what are you going to do about Nadzia?"

"I'm going to stop her from passing any more information to the Russians."

"How are you going to do that?"

"I don't know. I could get her deported."

"Promise you won't kill her."

"I will if I have to."

"There's no reason why you would have to. You could always do what I did. You could follow her and make sure she doesn't give anything to the Russians."

"I could do that," he agreed.

When he returned to the apartment the next day, he looked as if something had gone wrong.

"What happened?" she asked him. They were in the kitchen, where she was making a grocery list.

"I killed Nadzia," he confessed, gazing at her hopelessly.

"Oh, no," she said, hoping it wasn't true. But she could tell from his face that it was, and she was immediately overwhelmed by a feeling of responsibility.

"I didn't intend to kill her," Marek said in his defense. "I went to see her, and I told her that if she didn't leave the country I'd have her deported."

"You went to her apartment?"

"I stood on the street for a while, as you did, but I got tired of waiting for her, so I went in and confronted her."

"What did you tell her?"

"I told her I knew what she was doing."

"Did she ask you how you knew?"

"She guessed. She remembered seeing a woman in a hood watching her and coming into the pastry shop when she was with those Russian men, and then she figured out who it was. She said that if I did anything to her, she would have you killed."

"Why me?" she asked, though she already knew.

"You're the only person who has evidence against her, the only person who can connect her with the murders of Czeslaw and Lukasz."

"Well, you could have gone to the police."

"I didn't want to leave her, and I couldn't make her go with me." He paused and took a deep breath. "I found a clothesline, and I was going to tie her up so she wouldn't go anywhere. But she resisted, and while I was trying to pin her arms behind her back she told me there was no way I could stop her from having you killed. Whatever I did to her, she would find a way to tell the Russians about you, and they would take care of it."

"Because I could connect them with the murders?"

"You're the only person who could. But if they don't know about you, then you'll be safe."

"So you killed her to stop her from telling them about me?"

"I wasn't going to kill her. I was only going to tie her up. But then she said I had no right to blame other people for what happened. It was my fault for being so naïve, for trusting people I never should have trusted."

"Who did she mean?"

"The CIA," Marek murmured.

"How did she know they betrayed you?"

"She worked for them."

"Mother of God," Eva said, bringing her hand to her mouth as if to stop the heave from her stomach.

"After telling me this she looked at me like I was a fool, a stupid fool, and I couldn't stand it. I grabbed her by the throat, and I choked her to death."

Eva went to her husband and put her arms around him. She held him tight while he sobbed like a baby. And she asked God to forgive them.

ELEVEN

EVA WAS NOW forced to question a fundamental assumption about herself. She already knew she wasn't a saint, but she had believed that she was a good person, and that by following the way of St. Thérèse she could express her love of God by doing little things. Now she had to admit the fact that by trying to do a big thing, she had caused the death of a human being. Granted, that woman wasn't an innocent bystander, but she was still a human being.

Over and over Eva had to confront the irrefutable argument that if she hadn't followed Nadzia, she wouldn't have seen her with the two Russian men, and she wouldn't have been able to tell Marek what she had seen. If she hadn't gotten involved, then Marek wouldn't have had a motive for killing Nadzia.

Why had she found that woman and followed her? Was it only to protect her husband? Wasn't it also because of what she had seen that woman doing with Marek? Because of the look that woman had given her while straddling Marek?

Clearly, her motive hadn't been pure, but even if it had been pure she still would have been responsible for the death of that woman, and she still would have been responsible for putting her husband in a position where for her sake he committed murder. She simply couldn't pardon herself, not only for what she had done to Nadzia but also for what she had done to Marek. By getting involved in his war against the government of Poland, she had perverted his heart and jeopardized his soul.. She had driven him to commit murder.

The next morning she went to St. James and confessed her sin. She didn't go into the details. She just told the priest that she had caused her husband to kill someone. The priest recommended that she and her husband go to the police, but she had decided against that, and the priest didn't change her mind. She wasn't going to subject Marek to punishment from the legal system for something that had been her fault. And she couldn't turn herself in without involving him.

On her way home she bought a newspaper, and in the kitchen she scanned it for news of the murder. There was nothing about it, and there was nothing about it the next day, which made her wonder if they had found the woman's body, or if the police were setting a trap to catch the killer.

After several days her preoccupation with Nadzia's death was interrupted by the news of her father's death. Her mother called her to tell her about it, and the next day she was on a flight to New York. It seemed like the longest flight she had ever taken.

That evening she sat at the kitchen table with her mother and talked about her father.

"It happened sooner than the doctor expected," her mother told her. "When your father heard about what happened in Poland, I think he gave up."

"You mean he gave up hope."

"Yes. When you were here in September, you gave him hope. He read the papers every day, looking for news about Poland. And then he read about the martial law."

"I understand," Eva said, wanting to share her feelings with her mother. "It affected Marek the same way."

"How is he?" her mother asked.

"He's really upset about what happened. He tried to stop it."

"I thought he was only involved in the debt problem."

"He was involved in more than that."

"Well, I understand why you couldn't tell me."

"I can tell you now. It doesn't matter. Marek was working for the CIA. He was trying to overthrow the communist government."

"Did you tell your father that?"

"I did. I asked him not to tell anyone."

"He didn't. He didn't even tell me."

"Well, Marek believed that the CIA wanted an independent, democratic Poland, just as he did. But they didn't. They wanted a military government. And they betrayed him."

"That must have been hard on him."

"It was. He blames himself for trusting them—and for trusting a woman who worked for both sides. She was giving information to the Russians, who killed two Polish student leaders, and I was afraid that they would kill Marek. I got involved, and I tried to protect him. I gave him evidence that she had betrayed him, and when he confronted her, she threatened to have me killed. So he killed her to protect me."

"Marek believed she could have you killed?"

"Oh, yes. And she could have. She had those students killed. I mean by telling the Russians about them."

"So you got involved because you were afraid that the Russians would kill Marek?"

"That was my main reason for acting."

"What was your other reason?"

Eva swallowed hard. "I caught Marek in bed with her."

"Oh, no," her mother said. "I'm so sorry."

That was what the people had said at the wake.

"So my motive for acting wasn't pure."

"Our motives are never pure."

"But I expected more of myself."

"You expected too much. You had the standards of a saint."

"I'm not a saint. I'm so much worse than I thought I was. I hate myself."

"You should hate what you did but not yourself."

"But I can never forgive myself."

"God gave you the ability to forgive."

"You mean the ability to forgive others."

"He also gave you the ability to forgive yourself. So use it."

"I'll try," Eva said. "But maybe I should start by trying to forgive that woman."

"Have you forgiven Marek?"

"Oh, yes. I always forgive him."

"I hope you made it clear to him that having sex with other women was unacceptable."

"I did. I know he'll never do that again."

"He better not," her mother said protectively.

As she lay in bed that night thinking about this conversation, she was impressed by the way her mother had accepted the fact that a human being had been killed. Her mother had acted as if such things happened in the normal course of life.

The funeral at St. Casimir was attended by a large number of people from the Polish community, and a long line of cars followed the hearse to Calvary Cemetery. Standing at the graveside next to her mother, Eva was overcome by sorrow, and all she could do was silently ask her father to forgive her. Now that she knew what she herself was capable of doing, she saw how presumptuous she had been to judge him.

As they lowered the coffin into the grave her mother put an arm around her and told her: "When you were born you made him so happy. You were his *polska dziewczynka*. And you'll always be his Polish girl."

After the burial there was a reception at the Polish-American Club, where people lined up at serving dishes of kielbasa, sauerkraut, pierogi, and potato pancakes. Eva had already talked with all these people at the wake, which had extended over two days with an afternoon shift and a night shift, so she sat down at a table with her mother and brothers, renouncing the food. As she looked around she saw everything differently now, including her brothers. If it weren't for an accident of birth, her brothers could have been Czeslaw or Lukasz.

Four days later she returned to London. She had done a lot of thinking on the flight, and as soon as she sat down with Marek in the living room she said: "Now that you no longer work for the CIA, I don't see any reason for us to stay here."

"I still work for the bank," he said.

"Is that a real job?"

"Of course it's a real job. When I go to Poland I always work on the foreign debt."

"Is that enough to keep you busy?"

"It's enough for the bank to keep me on its staff."

"Well, it's not enough for me. I mean, it's not enough for me to go to class and have lunch with Juliana. I need to work. If we stay here, I'm going to start the orientation in January."

"I think that's a good idea."

She took a sip of wine, which he had poured for her. "Have you heard from the police?"

"About what?"

"About that woman."

"No. Why should I have heard from them?"

"I thought they might be able to connect you with her."

"There's no way they could," he assured her. "They don't know anything about her."

"You mean they couldn't identify her?"

"She had no papers. She was here illegally."

"What did they do with her body?"

"I don't know. I guess they cremated it."

Relieved, she returned to her main question. "Are we going to stay here just so you can work on Poland's foreign debt?"

"It's not just for that. I'll be doing something else."

"I hope you won't be working for the CIA."

"No. I'll be working on my own."

"You can't do anything on your own."

"I can do more than I could working for them. I'm in contact with our leaders in Poland, and I'm trying to revive the plan of overthrowing the government."

"I thought the leaders had all been arrested."

"Most of them have been. But some of them are still at large, and I believe we still have a chance of overthrowing Jaruzelski."

"So you're not going to give up on this."

"I'm never going to give up on it."

She sighed. "All right. Then we'll stay in London."

They celebrated Christmas Eve at a Polish restaurant in Balham. She would have preferred a neighborhood that didn't remind her of what she had done, but she knew she would never forget it, so there was no point in trying to avoid it.

Surrounded by Polish exiles observing their traditions in a strange land, she connected with her heritage and remembered celebrating *Wigilia* with her family, passing around the *opłatek* and breaking off small pieces and exchanging them as a symbol of love and forgiveness.

Handing a piece of the wafer to her husband, Eva wished him: *"Zdrowia, szczęścia, a Pan błogosławi."*

"Tym samym dla ciebie," Marek said.

The restaurant served the traditional meatless meal, including mushroom soup, pickled herring, pierogi filled with potatoes and cheese, noodles with poppy seeds, sauerkraut, and fried carp. An extra place was set at their table for the unexpected guest.

They lingered after dinner to hear a choir sing *kolędy*, the Polish Christmas carols they always sang in St. Casimir at midnight mass. She would have liked to go to midnight mass at the nearby Polish church, but she knew that Marek wouldn't go with her, so she settled for singing softly along with the carol *"Dzisiaj w Betlejem,"* remembering happy times with her family and realizing what she had lost.

Resigned to staying in London, she started the orientation for a nursing license in January. At the same time she started another course at Birkbeck. It was in the evening, so it didn't conflict with the orientation.

She was happy to see Francis at the first class, and since Marek was on a trip to Poland they had dinner at the Irish pub.

"There haven't been any bombs since October," Eva said when they had ordered.

"No. There haven't been," Francis said thankfully.

"They must be listening to you."

"Either that or they're out of explosives."

"I assume you've been following the situation in Poland."

"I have, and I'm sorry. I was hoping they'd have a peaceful revolution."

"My husband still thinks they could have a revolution, but it might not be peaceful."

"If it's not, then it will only lead to more violence."

"I know what you mean. I got involved in the situation, and I caused the death of someone."

"Tell me about it," he said calmly.

"I already told a priest about it. I made a confession, but I didn't give him all the details. I don't know why. I never held back before."

"Maybe you didn't have anything to hold back."

"You're right. I didn't. I thought I'd committed major sins, but all I'd done was quarrel with my brothers or not help my mother enough."

"You were holding yourself to high standards."

"My model was St. Thérèse of Lisieux. It still is, but now I can see that the major sins she thought she committed were like the sins I committed as a girl."

"They were minor sins."

"They were little sins," Eva agreed, "consistent with her Little Way. And if I hadn't deviated from that way, I wouldn't have committed a big sin."

"What did you do?"

She told him the whole story of Nadzia.

He listened without interrupting her, encouraging her silently to keep going until she had given him all the details, and then he said: "You were trying to protect your husband. And you didn't know he was going to kill her."

"I asked him to promise not to kill her, so I must have known he was capable of killing her."

"We're all capable of killing people."

"Then what stops us?"

"Our love for God stops us."

"It wouldn't have stopped my husband. He's an atheist."

"Then his love for you should have stopped him."

"But his love for me made him kill her."

"Are you sure about that?"

"Yes. I am. We both acted out of love for the other."

After a moment Francis said: "I believe you acted out of love for him. Of course, as you say, your motive wasn't pure. You wanted to protect him, but you were also angry at her because she had threatened your marriage. But you didn't want to hurt her. You only wanted to stop her from hurting him."

"And he wanted to stop her from hurting me."

"I'm not seeing that. I'm seeing that he used her to test your love for him."

"I know he did. But I know why he had to test my love, so I don't blame him."

"I'm not suggesting that you should blame him."

"Then what are you suggesting?"

"I'm suggesting that you should question his love for you."

"Why should I question it?"

"Because of the way he abuses you."

"He doesn't abuse me," Eva insisted. "He tests me."

"Whatever you want to call it," Francis said, "he abuses you."

"He doesn't do it to hurt me."

"But it does hurt you."

"I still believe he loves me."

"When you love people, you think about them. But he thinks only about himself."

"How do you know?"

"I know from what you've just told me about him," Francis said. "Your husband's incapable of thinking about other people. He's like a child who sees the world as an extension of himself. He doesn't know the meaning of love."

"Well, I don't see how you can say that about him," Eva said defensively. "You haven't even met him."

"I don't have to meet him. I've met enough people like him."

"You mean the people who plant bombs?"

"Yes. They're not thinking about other people. They're not thinking about Ireland. They're thinking only about themselves."

"So you think my husband doesn't love me?"

Francis nodded. "He needs you, but he doesn't love you. And since his need is bottomless, you can never satisfy it."

"If I love him enough, I can."

"No. You never can."

Their food arrived, and they were silent for a while.

"If he hadn't used that woman to test me," Eva said, "they wouldn't have found out what he was doing."

"That might explain why he killed her," Francis said. "He was angry at himself for letting his need interfere with his mission, but instead of accepting responsibility, he blamed her. So he didn't kill her to protect you. He killed her to protect himself."

"From what?"

"From the truth."

Eva understood. "Well, that makes me feel a little better, but it doesn't absolve me."

"It doesn't absolve you," Francis agreed. "You'll have to work that out with God. And I believe you'll be able to because there are no limits to God's mercy."

"I gather that you don't believe I'll be able to work things out with my husband."

"All things are possible, but I don't believe it's likely."

"Then what can I do?"

"You can stop trying to pass his tests."

"But if I didn't pass a test, then he'd be lost."

"If he wants to be lost, then you can't save him."

"He doesn't want to be lost," she said, remembering what he had said to her in the Recovery Room. "He wants to be saved."

Francis shook his head. "From what you told me, I'm not seeing that. I'm seeing a person who wants to drive you beyond your limit."

"For what purpose?"

"To validate his feelings."

"About what?"

"About himself. It's all about him. The world, Poland, your marriage—they're all about him. He's the only character in the drama. Even God doesn't have a role."

"Well, I have a role," Eva said.

"Unfortunately, you do. You're the stand-in for God. And I'm advising you as a friend to reject that role."

"Thank you. I appreciate it."

The next morning she went to mass at St. James, and she spent the rest of the morning walking around, thinking about what Francis had said. She had never questioned whether Marek loved her, and now she did. She acknowledged the point that Francis had made about the way Marek treated her. She could see how by testing her love he had abused her. And she could see how he might need her more than he loved her. But she still believed that he wanted to be saved. She couldn't believe that he was simply using her to validate his feelings about himself.

As she wandered the streets of Marylebone she wondered what would happen if she did what Francis had advised. If she stopped trying to pass her husband's tests, would he really be lost? Could she be ascribing to herself a power that no human being had? Was she being arrogant in believing that she could save him? Was she enabling his weakness by loving him and forgiving him no matter what he did?

Well, at least she had drawn a line. She had made it clear that she would leave him if he ever cheated on her again. But now he had killed someone. Was that another test of her love? Had she passed that test because she felt responsible?

But what if Francis was right about why Marek had killed that woman? What if he had killed her for betraying him, for giving the Russians information that had doomed his effort to liberate Poland? What if he had killed her because he blamed himself for getting involved with her and giving her the opportunity to betray him? What if it *was* all about him? Should she draw another line with him? Should she make it clear that she wouldn't put up with any more tests?

After struggling with these questions she asked God to help her with the answers. She asked the Blessed Mother, St. Thérèse, and all the other saints that she could remember to help her understand the situation.

Around noon she took the tube to Balham and walked to the street where Nadzia had lived. She stood in front of the fateful house with her head bare and the wind in her face, confronting the fact of the woman's death. With her jacket open she let the cold penetrate to her bones. And over and over, staring at the house, she murmured an act of contrition: "O my God, I am sorry for my sins because I have offended you. I know I should love you above all things. Help me to do penance, to do better, and to avoid anything that might lead me to sin. Amen."

After numerous repetitions she left the spot and walked to Balham High Road. She stopped in front of the pastry shop, remembering how she had seen Nadzia at the table with the two Russians, and how she had gone into the shop to spy on them.

"*O mój Boże,*" she began again, oblivious of the people walking by her. "*Zmiłuj się nade mną.*"

As she walked to the Balham station she decided to make a trip here two or three times a week as an act of penance.

On the way home from the Baker Street station she bought some groceries. She didn't need many things since she had only herself to feed. She didn't know when Marek would return, but she hadn't heard from him, so she didn't expect him back that day. And she didn't have those boys to feed, those poor starving students.

As she climbed the stairs to the apartment she was worrying about Marek, who she assumed was meeting with people who had gone underground. So she was more than surprised to see him when she opened the door to the apartment.

He was sitting in one of the chairs that faced the sofa. In fact, he was tied to the chair, with a rope around him and his hands behind the back of the chair.

Then she saw the two Russian men, one on the sofa and the other standing in the doorway to the kitchen. They weren't wearing overcoats and hats, but they looked like the two men she had seen in the pastry shop with Nadzia.

"We were wondering where you were," the one on the sofa said in Polish with an accent.

"We expected you to come home sooner," the other one said.

Marek looked at her helplessly.

"What do you want?" she asked them.

"We want information from your husband."

"He doesn't have any information. He's only a banker."

"We know he just came back from Poland, where he was meeting with opposition leaders."

"I don't know anything you don't already know," Marek said.

"We think you do. And if you don't tell us everything, we're going to kill you."

"I don't care if you kill me. But don't touch my wife."

"I was just wondering," the man in the kitchen doorway said, "what it would be like to touch your wife. She's very attractive."

"I'm warning you," Marek said furiously.

"You're not in any position to warn us," the man on the sofa said. "You have one minute to start telling us what you did in Poland."

The other man raised a hand that was holding a gun, which he pointed at Eva. "If you don't, then we'll kill your wife."

TWELVE

"ALL RIGHT," MAREK said. "I'll tell you what I did."

The man in the kitchen doorway lowered the gun, but he kept his lascivious eyes on Eva as if he were still wondering what it would be like to touch her.

"I met with union leaders, and we talked about organizing a general strike."

"Where did you meet with them?"

"In Warsaw and Gdańsk."

"Give us their names."

He gave them names, which to Eva sounded as if he had made them up. In fact, they were translations of American rock stars, but they evidently fooled the Russians.

"Who else did you meet with?"

"Student leaders. We talked about organizing a demonstration."

"Give us their names."

He gave them more names, which were more translations of rock stars and also film stars.

"What else did you do there?"

"Nothing. That's it."

"Then we have no further use for you," the man on the sofa said coldly.

The other man raised the gun and pointed it at Marek. "We should kill you right now, but we'll let you go on one condition."

"What's that?"

"Give us your wife."

"What do you mean?" Marek said, looking alarmed.

"Tell her she should make us happy."

"No. I won't. My wife isn't a whore like Nadzia."

"Then you better say a prayer," the man with the gun said, extending it toward Marek.

"Wait," Eva said, accepting the fact that there was only one way she could save him. "What do you want from me?"

"I think you can guess."

"Don't do it," Marek said. "They're going to kill me anyway."

If they killed him they would kill her, so she had nothing to lose. "I'll do whatever you say."

"*Horosho*. Kneel down on the floor."

She did as she was ordered.

"Now, bend forward and raise your skirt."

When they had gone she picked herself up from the floor and went to Marek and untied him.

"Did they hurt you?" he asked as if he didn't know.

She only said: "I need to go to the hospital."

He held her arm as they went down the stairs and out to the street, where they looked for a taxi.

Luckily, it didn't take long to spot one.

The taxi took them to the nearest hospital, where she was received in the emergency room.

The doctor, a woman, examined her with controlled anger. "Who did this to you?"

"Two men," Eva said through gritted teeth.

"Could you identify them?"

"I guess I could."

"Where did it happen?"

"In our apartment."

"Was your husband there at the time?"

"No. He was at work."

"How did the men get into your apartment?"

"They were waiting for me on the stairs. They had a gun."

"Well, you should report it to the police."

"Do I have to?"

"No. But don't be afraid to."

"That's easy to say," she murmured, wincing as the doctor swabbed her with disinfectant.

"Does your husband know what happened to you?"

"No," she said truthfully. Though he had watched it, he had no idea what it had been like being raped by those barbarians.

"Are you going to tell him?"

"I don't know. I have to think about it."

"Well, at least there's almost no risk that you'll get pregnant."

"Dziękuję Bogu," Eva said, closing her eyes.

When they got home she went straight to bed. The doctor had given her something for the pain, but that wasn't the worst of it. What made her cry was the fact that her body, a temple of the Holy Spirit, had been violated. Though she had let it happen to save her husband's life, she had lost her integrity and her self-respect. And she felt degraded.

"Can I get you anything?" Marek asked solicitously.

"No, thanks. I just need to rest."

"How do you feel?"

"I feel like shit."

"I'm sorry."

Wanting to put it in terms that he could understand, she said: "I feel like Poland after it was taken by the Russians."

"I'll get those bastards."

"Please don't."

"I can't let them get away with it."

"Yes, you can. You can stop the violence."

"You mean I should forgive them for what they did?"

"You should try to forgive them. The pope forgave the man who shot him."

"I'm not the pope. And what about you? Are you going to forgive those bastards?"

"I'm going to try. It won't be easy, but I'm going to try."

"You know," he said after a moment. "You saved my life."

She remembered what Francis had said about Marek: whatever happened, it was about him, it was only about him. "Actually, I saved both our lives."

"Oh, they wouldn't have killed you."

"They would have killed you and left me as a witness?"

"Well, I guess they wouldn't have," he said as if it hadn't occurred to him. "In any case you proved that you love me."

Wondering if she had proved anything, she said: "Please leave me alone. I need to rest."

The next morning she went to the Lady Chapel and prayed. She had an issue with God now, a big issue. Why had he let those men rape her? She had always kept her body pure. She hadn't had sex with anyone except her husband. She hadn't used the pill. She hadn't even used the rhythm method to avoid getting pregnant. She had wanted a baby. She had wanted more than one baby. So why had God punished her this way?

As if in reply the face of Nadzia was superimposed on the face of the Blessed Mother. That explained it. God had punished her for having caused the death of that woman, for not being sorry enough, and for not doing enough penance.

But what did God expect her to do? Go to the police and implicate her husband? Betray her husband? Send him to jail for something that was really her fault?

She could never do that to her husband. She could only accept the punishment that God had inflicted on her, trusting in His ultimate mercy. She could only keep telling God how sorry she was and doing penance and asking for His forgiveness.

"*O mój Boże,*" she said, beginning an act of contrition.

When she left the chapel she decided to go to Balham as a way of continuing her penance. She took the tube to Balham station and walked to the street where Nadzia had lived. Again, she stood in front of the house and repented her sin. She accepted the pain where the Russians had forced their way into her as if it was a just punishment.

Then, as she had the previous day, she walked back to Balham High Road and stopped in front of the pastry shop. Inside, at the table in the corner, she saw the two Russian men with Nadzia— and her husband.

Marek was laughing about something with them.

A cry of shock and recognition arose from her throat. Her view of what had happened to her was shattered into the pieces, which in a flash came together in a whole new pattern. She wasn't responsible for the death of anyone, and she hadn't been punished by God for what she had done. She had been abused by her husband.

Instead of confronting him in the shop, she fled the scene and found refuge in the Polish church where they had held the memorial service for Czeslaw. It reminded her of St. Casimir, and it made her feel like she was home.

In a rear pew near a side aisle she knelt down and thanked God for revealing the truth to her. She thanked Him for the fact that she wouldn't have to go through life with the burden of thinking she had caused the death of that woman. She thanked Him for Ramona and Juliana and Francis, who had helped her make sense of what she had witnessed in the pastry shop. And she thanked Him for showing her the way back to her mission in life.

She was waiting for Marek when he got home.

"*Ty dupku,*" she snarled, slapping his face as hard as she could.

"What's that for?" he asked, surprised.

"It's for making a game out of our marriage."

"I didn't make a game out of it."

"You didn't, uh? Then what do you call pretending that you killed that woman?"

"I didn't pretend. I really did kill her."

"And what do you call pretending that those Russian men were going to kill you?"

"I wasn't pretending. They really were going to kill me."

"Stop lying to me. I *saw* you with them in the pastry shop."

"You did?" he said, looking caught. "When?"

"Today," she said. "You were sitting at a table with them. You were *laughing* with them."

"I wasn't laughing."

"You *were* laughing. I saw you."

"I'm sorry," he said, advancing toward her.

"Don't come any closer."

He stopped. "I was just testing your love for me."

"You didn't have to test it. And you didn't have to hurt me the way you did. Have you any idea how I felt allowing those brutes to ram their way into me?"

"I can imagine."

"You can't imagine. You can't imagine anything unless it's about you."

"I have a reason for being what I am."

"We all have a reason for being what we are, but some of us try to overcome it."

"Well, I warned you," he said, pleading his case. "You knew what you were getting into."

"I didn't know. I thought I did. And that was my fault."

"You said you'd love me no matter what I did."

"I believed that, but I never imagined that you were capable of doing what you did."

"I couldn't help it. I had to test you more and more."

"Until you drove me beyond my limit."

"So what are you going to do now?"

"I'm going to leave you. I'm on a flight tomorrow afternoon."

"I thought divorce wasn't allowed by your religion."

"It isn't, but annulment is."

"You mean if you pay them enough money."

"I don't know much about the process. I never thought it would happen to me."

"It hasn't happened yet. We have until tomorrow afternoon to talk about it."

"No, we don't. I'm going to spend the night with Juliana."

"You've already packed?"

"I've packed everything I want to take with me."

"Don't leave me," he begged her, giving her the look he had given her in the Recovery Room. "If you do, I'll be lost."

"I can't save you. Only God can save you."

"I don't believe in God."

"That's *your* problem, not mine."

Within a few minutes she was going down the stairs with her two suitcases. He hadn't offered to help her with them, and even if he had she wouldn't have accepted the offer. Carrying her own suitcases was a declaration of independence.

She spent the night with Juliana, who wasn't surprised by her decision to leave Marek and didn't need to know the details. By now Eva understood that her friends had been able to see things about him that she hadn't been able to see, not because they were more perceptive but because they weren't in love with him. Evidently, it was true: love was blind.

Ramona was at the airport to meet her, and they came together in a long hug when Eva finally emerged from customs with her suitcases.

"Welcome home," Ramona said with tears in her eyes.

"Seeing you, I feel like I'm home," Eva said.

Without another word Ramona took one of her suitcases, and they went to find a taxi.

No one had occupied her bedroom since Eva had moved into Marek's apartment as his wife, so it was ready for her. Ramona had cleaned it for her and put a dozen yellow roses in a vase on the chest of drawers.

They had *arroz con pollo* for dinner, and they talked long into the night. Eva told her friend what had happened but without going into every gory detail.

The next day she walked over to New York Hospital, and within a few days she was back at her old job on the pediatrics floor. She was as happy being a nurse as she had been before, except that now, after a year of not being able to practice, she had a deeper appreciation of her profession.

As soon as she was settled she called her mother.

"I'm back in New York," she told her mother after the usual preliminaries. "I'm working at my old job at the hospital."

"Where's Marek?" her mother asked as if she had guessed he wasn't with her.

"He's still in London, still trying to save his country."

"Did you leave him?"

"I did. I'm going to try to get an annulment."

"So you reached your limit."

"I went beyond it."

"Well, now you know you have a limit."

"I learned the hard way."

"We all learn the hard way," her mother said. "And don't feel responsible for him."

"I won't. I realize now," Eva said, "that there's a limit not only on my love, but also on my responsibility."

"I'm glad you realize that. I think you had an overextended sense of responsibility."

"Why didn't you tell me?"

"I did tell you. But you wanted to be a saint."

"I guess I did. But I don't want to be a saint anymore. I only want to be a good human being."

"You already are a good human being."

"Kocham cię, mama."

"Kocham cię też."

A few days after she had begun the process of getting an annulment she was informed by the bank that Marek had been killed in Poland. She was saddened by his death, and she grieved for him, but she didn't feel responsible.

Fulfilling her duty as his wife she took the long flight to Warsaw, where she identified his body in the morgue. His father, a professorial man who didn't look a bit like his son, arrived in time to make a decision about what to do with Marek's remains. They agreed that he would want his body cremated and his ashes scattered in the harbor of Gdańsk, the birthplace of Solidarity, so they went by train to the old city.

In the last light of day they walked out onto a pier and stood at the edge, with Eva holding the container of ashes. She closed her eyes and prayed for Marek's immortal soul, and then she opened the container. Shaking out the ashes, she found a place in her heart to forgive him, and watching them fall upon the dark water, she felt a profound sense of relief.

She thanked God for keeping Marek alive until after she had left him, until after she had begun the process of separation. Now with his death, she was separated not only from him but also from the girl who had believed that she could save people by loving them. That girl had died, and now reborn, she could let fall a shower of roses.

BOOK CLUB GUIDE TO

A Shower of Roses

Tom Milton

An introduction to *A Shower of Roses*

Eva Koziol grew up in St. Paul, Minnesota, the daughter of two displaced persons who barely escaped from Poland at the end of World War II. Though her father had a university education, he worked in a refrigerator plant due to his lack of proficiency in English, while her mother, who had been a nurse in Poland, eventually qualified for that profession in America. Outside of their work and their children, their lives were delimited by St. Casimir's Church and the Polish-American Center.

Once she reached a certain age, Eva began to break away from her ethnic roots, and among other things, she swore she would never marry a Polish man. She found her mission early in life from reading the works of St. Thérèse of Lisieux, who became her patron saint and showed her how she could help people by doing little things for them, instead of performing great heroic acts. She put that mission into action by pursuing a career as a nurse.

She was in her last semester of nursing school when she saw her father go into a sleazy hotel with a woman who was not her mother, and not being able to deal with the knowledge that her father was cheating on her mother, presumably without her mother being aware of it, she left St. Paul and got a nursing job in New York. She worked on the pediatrics floor of a large hospital and shared an apartment with a colleague, a woman named Ramona, who had Puerto Rican parents and grew up in the Barrio around 116th Street. She began to learn Spanish from Ramona, which helped her communicate with her patients, and they became close friends. Like other single women their age, they went to bars in their neighborhood with the idea of meeting suitable men.

Things were going well for Eva, who along with Ramona had just completed her bachelor's in nursing at Hunter College, when she met Marek, a Polish exile, in a bar and fell in love with him. Marek ostensibly worked for a large international bank, but that was only a cover for his role as a CIA agent with the mission of fomenting a popular uprising against the communist government of Poland. Eva found out about Marek's real occupation after making what for her was an irrevocable commitment to him, but she accepted the situation, and she married him with the blessing of her parents, who were happy that he was Polish.

A few months after the wedding, at the request of the CIA, the bank transferred Marek to London so that he would be closer to the action. The story opens a few months later, in April 1981, shortly after Poland announced that it would be unable to repay its foreign debt and the Solidarity movement emerged in the port of Gdańsk. Eva has begun the process of becoming licensed as a nurse in England, but in the meantime she has nothing to do. She has one friend, Juliana, a woman from Brazil who is married to a lawyer whose firm has Marek's bank as a client. Juliana's father, an apolitical obstetrician, had to send her out of Brazil because as a student she had gotten into trouble with the military government. So, like Marek, she is an exile.

To occupy her time Eva takes a graduate course in human development at the University of London, where she meets Francis, a young priest from Ireland who serves the Irish community in London, including members of the IRA who are planting bombs at city landmarks. In talking with Francis, she begins to see the similarities between the situations in Poland and Northern Ireland.

Juliana and Francis give Eva some different perspectives on her situation, and they help her understand the problems in her marriage. She is fully aware that her husband's work is dangerous, and every time he goes to Poland she worries that he will be arrested by the secret police. But she devotes her life to him, and though he drags her into a world of political intrigue and tests her love by subjecting her to increasingly painful experiences, she keeps her promise to love him no matter what he does, until she confronts the truth about him—and about herself.

A conversation with Tom Milton

In your first four novels you gave us strong, principled women as heroines, and we saw them from the point of view of admiring male narrators. In this novel the heroine is the narrator, and the point of view is female. Did you have a reason for this change?

I felt that with this heroine, who is self-reflective, I had to get closer to the character, and I had to strip away the film of admiration. We see Eva through her own eyes, and she can be very tough on herself.

She certainly applies high standards to herself. When she was young she wanted to be a saint, and at times I feel that she hasn't completely let go of that ambition.

In a sense, you're right. She still believes in the power of her love to save another human being.

When she falls in love with Marek, there's a physical attraction, and there's also his bottomless need for love, which she responds to. But I wonder if there isn't also a challenge. I mean, I wonder if she senses that of all the people in the world, Marek would be the hardest to save.

I think she knows he'll be a challenge, but I don't think she knows the extent of Marek's predicament. She's seen something like it before in her father, but what happened to her father and what happened to Marek are quite different.

Her father lost his family in a war, while Marek was abandoned by his mother when he was a baby. From what I know about psychology, I believe the latter has much deeper effects on people.

Much deeper. Marek's mother consciously abandoned him, and she made sure that he couldn't find her. Those of us who weren't abandoned by our mothers can only imagine what that's like. And even then, we really don't know.

We see Eva at an early age wanting to make her father happy and thinking she can't, no matter what she does.

She can't undo what happened to her father. Ironically, she believes that the only thing she ever did that made her father happy was marrying Marek.

After swearing she would never marry a Polish man.

In that respect I think Eva is typical of girls in close ethnic communities. They feel stifled, they want to get out, and the last thing they want to do is marry someone from that community.

It's a healthy reaction. It has the function of avoiding marriages between people who are too close genetically.

Or too close culturally.

Even though he's Polish, Marek isn't like any man Eva ever met before. He's not at all like the young men her parents wanted her to marry. So why aren't they more leery of him?

He's what her father wishes he still could be. But her mother does have concerns about not knowing his parents.

Let's talk about Eva's mission, which she got from her readings of St. Thérèse of Lisieux. She's content with doing little things to help people, whereas Marek aspires to doing big things. Is there a gender angle here?

There's no intended gender angle. In fact, in my first four novels I show women doing things that most men would be afraid to do, while the male narrators mostly watch them. It's really about what an individual like Eva would do, or what an individual like Marek would do. Their different missions are in their natures, not in their genders.

You mean they're doing what comes naturally, not what they were programmed to do. And it's interesting that when Eva deviates from her mission and tries to do a big thing, she gets into trouble.

She's out of her element.

Like your other heroines, Eva is committed to nonviolence, and she wonders if she could love Marek if he killed someone.

She wonders, but she's committed to loving him no matter what he does, so if he does kill someone she still has to love him. Her love for Marek is unconditional.

Like you I was brought up to believe that we should love other people as God loves us. But how can we possibly do that? We're only human. Surely, our love has limits to it.

That's a question I'm exploring in this novel. Eva believes that her love for Marek has no limit, even though her mother has told her that human love does have limits.

Marek keeps testing her love for him, and each time the test gets harder. What's he trying to prove?

He could be trying to prove that he's unworthy of love, which would validate the feelings he has about himself. Or he could be trying to prove that Eva is a saint.

Don't you know?

I think I know. But as I said, we can only imagine how being abandoned by their mothers affects people.

Discussion questions

1. Why was Eva attracted to the mission of helping people by doing little things for them?

2. Why did Eva respond to the discovery of her father's infidelity the way she did?

3. What do Eva and Ramona have in common other than the fact that they are pediatric nurses at the same hospital?

4. What does Eva learn by sharing with Ramona her discovery about her father?

5. How does Eva's experience with her father make her susceptible to Marek's appeal in the Recovery Room?

6. What makes Eva believe that she can love Marek no matter what he does?

7. What do Eva and Juliana have in common other than the fact that their husbands are involved in international banking?

8. What important insights about herself does Eva gain from her conversations with Juliana?

9. In one conversation with Juliana, Eva talks about the Jungian concept of reconciling the past and the future. Why is Eva unable to do this?

10. What do Eva and Francis have in common other than the fact that they are both taking the same course at the University of London?

11. What important insights about her husband does Eva gain from her conversations with Francis?

12. Did Marek's personal needs jeopardize his political mission?

13. Why does Eva trust Marek and believe everything he says?

14. Is Eva's commitment to her mission compromised by her devotion to her husband?

15. While Marek is testing Eva's love for him, is he also testing her faith in God?

16. Who do you think betrayed Marek?

17. Do you think what happens to Eva supports the notion that in spite of all the advice we get from other people, we can learn only from our own experience?